THE KINGDOM CHANGED

A novel by

SUNNY ABAKWUE

Gotham Books

30 N Gould St.
Ste. 20820, Sheridan, WY 82801
https://gothambooksinc.com/

Phone: 1 (307) 464-7800

© 2025 *Sunny Abakwue*. All rights reserved.

No part of this book may be reproduced, stored in a retrieval system, or transmitted by any means without the written permission of the author.

Published by Gotham Books (May 22, 2025)

ISBN: 979-8-3493-3539-6 (H)
ISBN: 979-8-3493-3537-2 (P)
ISBN: 979-8-3493-3538-9 (E)

Because of the dynamic nature of the Internet, any web addresses or links contained in this book may have changed since publication and may no longer be valid.

The views expressed in this work are solely those of the author and do not necessarily reflect the views of the publisher, and the publisher hereby disclaims any responsibility for them.

TABLE OF CONTENTS

CHAPTER ONE 1
CHAPTER TWO 7
CHAPTER THREE 14
CHAPTER FOUR 21
CHAPTER FIVE 31
CHAPTER FIVE (B) 37
CHAPTER FIVE (C) 43
CHAPTER SIX 47
CHAPTER SEVEN 53
CHAPTER EIGHT 58
CHAPTER NINE 62
CHAPTER TEN 69
CHAPTER ELEVEN 74
CHAPTER TWELVE 80
CHAPTER THIRTEEN 91
CHAPTER FOURTEEN 94
CHAPTER FIFTEEN 102
CHAPTER FIFTEEN (B) 112
CHAPTER SIXTEEN 118
CHAPTER SEVENTEEN 129
CHAPTER SEVENTEEN (B) 136
CHAPTER EIGHTEEN 139
CHAPTER EIGHTEEN (B) 144
CHAPTER EIGHTEEN (C) 151
CHAPTER NINETEEN 155

CHAPTER NINETEEN (B)	159
CHAPTER NINETEEN (C)	161
CHAPTER TWENTY	165
CHAPTER TWENTY (B)	169
CHAPTER TWENTY (C)	175
CHAPTER TWENTY-ONE	178
CHAPTER TWENTY-ONE (B)	184
CHAPTER TWENTY-TWO	188
CHAPTER TWENTY-TWO (B)	192
CHAPTER TWENTY-THREE	197
CHAPTER TWENTY-THREE (B)	200
CHAPTER TWENTY-FOUR	203
CHAPTER TWENTY-FOUR (B)	207
CHAPTER TWENTY-FIVE	213
CHAPTER TWENTY-FIVE (B)	218
CHAPTER TWENTY-SIX	221
CHAPTER TWENTY-SIX (B)	230
CHAPTER TWENTY-SEVEN	239
CHAPTER TWENTY-EIGHT	248
CHAPTER TWENTY-NINE	255
CHAPTER TWENTY-NINE (B)	259
CHAPTER TWENTY-NINE (C)	265
CHAPTER THIRTY	271
CHAPTER THIRTY (B)	275
CHAPTER THIRTY (C)	280
CHAPTER THIRTY (D)	285
CHAPTER THIRTY-ONE	291
CHAPTER THIRTY-TWO	295
CHAPTER THIRTY-THREE	299

"The Spirit of the Lord sayest unto me … write"
                    In Author's Dream

CHAPTER ONE

Mr. Bingo was a hunter before he became the King – only to become a prodigal King after he took the Crown. From the early stage of his initiation into the customary rite of passage, it was self-evident that the hand of fate was upon him.

Mr. Bingo was born a poor man. Both his parents were claimed by that fearful messenger of fate which the early missionaries called, the "small pox". Had the hard wind of fate not dealt him an initial hard blow, he would have had a better understanding of what having parents, good parents for that matter, was all about.

Mr. Bingo lived his life, a hunter and a gatherer until one day a wicked witch of the village turned all her crafts against him. She wanted to kill him because his hunting expedition was taking him nearer and nearer to the Sacred Oracle, the core of wisdom for all Christians, Muslims and Animists.

For some time then, the members of the animists' temple were the privileged few who could draw nearer, even enter into the holy cave where the Holy Serpent was living. The resident of the cave, a colorful and a venerated python, was a hunter, too. And the holy hunter-python was a much better hunter that did not want other creatures, much less its worshippers, like mere human hunters, to hunt in its vast territory.

Naturally, however, Mr. Bingo was a hunter in the hand of destiny. The Great Oracle, the Benevolent Star of the King, was out to help him. For some time, then, the Great Oracle of the land was carefully searching for someone to be crowned a King of the Kingdom. Also, the same Oracle was, painstakingly looking for the man who would be the right fit for the Crown of the Kingdom. But the people of the vast Kingdom did not even know.

Mr. Bingo had a strange dream. In his dream he saw the evil witch of the Kingdom flying on a single broom trying to slay him. But behind the native witch was a colorful python, the type he had learnt and heard ruled the Kingdom, chasing, confusing and frustrating every effort of the witch who was determined to harm him. The nightmare lasted all night long.

When Mr. Bingo woke up on the following day, he knew that such a dream was a prelude to a mixed omen. Nature rather, an evil fate had played him a trick before. Besides, he knew from the words of the Sacred Sage that a dream with twisting proportion was not a trifle, but a fugue of dual events to come. He decided to pay a visit to the most outstanding medicine man who would reveal to him the significance of the whole dream.

Hardly did Mr. Bingo pay his dues when the Sacred Spirit of the Oracle made its appearance. The medicine-man was surprised when the voice of the Spirit forbade him from accepting the requisite dues.

"You must refund him all the charges you exacted from him, for he has found favor in my sight" said the Spirit firmly.

"I don't believe this" said Mr. Bingo in a total disbelief. The Sacred Spirit of the Oracle knew that he did not believe. That he had a genuine reason to back up his disbelief. After all, he was a mere hunter, a profession requisite for the peasant domain.

"Do not be misguided by your psychic agents. I have spoken. My words shall come to pass" the voice of the Sacred Spirit of the Oracle declared.

"Please the embodiment of our forefathers, our Supreme Oracle, when will your words come to pass?" Mr. Bingo asked with skepticism. He knew he could not outsmart the god of all gods, especially in its presence. He knew too he could not conceal the contents of his thoughts by venturing to argue with the Ultimate god.

"The King shall rule his people. And as the hunter is chosen, so shall he live to be the King. Depart ye in peace. My blessings shall abide with thee". Thus answered the voice of the Sacred Spirit of the Holy Oracle.

Away Mr. Bingo began to go. Beside him was the medicine-man who was blessed with the honor to know the future King before everyone else. Mr. Bingo touched his host on his shoulder. It was customary sign used in drawing a confidential attention.

"Please, speak your highness" the medicine man responded in a manner that reflected his total loyalty to the future King.

"It is one thing to make a promise, it is really another to fulfill it" said Mr. Bingo, thus confiding in the medicine man as the latter was escorting him from his compound.

"I am not sure the Sacred Spirit of the Great Oracle will like that" the medicine-man protested.

"I trust the Oracle, but I disbelieve confidence game". Mr. Bingo bared his mind, thus brushing off the protest.

"Please, Your Highness, be careful. The wind can carry a secret conversation" said the medicine -man.

"I have heard such rubbish before" responded Mr. Bingo.

Offended, the medicine man turned around and went back to his compound without saying another word.

While on his way to his own house Mr. Bingo decided to have a second opinion. He knew another Sacred Sage who was not only a medicine-man, a necromancer, a fortune-teller, but an astrologer as well. This man's name was Shaqouis Iptoquois. And he felt, perhaps he would reveal some hidden truths which the offended Sage did not, Mr. Bingo thought.

For sure he did reveal some truths – sad truths this time around – Truths in that Mr. Bingo's nagging disbelief had become a burdensome irritation to the otherwise Benevolent Spirit.

As soon as Sherman Shaqouis Iptoquois opened the door to his Sacred Shrine, the same Spirit of the Oracle made its presence known.

"To your door cometh a disbeliever, his name is Bingo, an ungrateful hunter. Charge him twice the normal dues" the Spirit commanded.

"I will" the Sherman Mr. Shaqouis Iptoquois replied, bowing his head in the process, lest the angry Spirit transfer his rage from the "disbeliever" unto him. In those days, as in nowadays, an enraged Spirit could throw a violent temper. A wise one, knowing what an angry Spirit could do, would be smart enough to stand away from the path of the flaming dart.

Mr. Bingo was at the gate, the entrance to the Sage's huge compound, when the angry Spirit gave its order to its Chief Priest.

A few moments later, the Chief Priest's messenger led the client, Mr. Bingo, to the door of the shrine. By this time the Spirit of the Oracle was no longer friendly.

"Come in Bingo. I spoke with you a while ago. But your disbelief will betray you" spoke the Spirit angrily. Mr. Bingo recognized the angry voice.

"I just wanted to…" Mr. Bingo began to give an excuse when the Spirit cut him off, completing his sentence in the process "to get a second opinion". The Spirit was no longer in the mood to pamper him again. To Mr. Bingo's horror and astonishment, the same old voice that came out the second Shrine saying "Behold a hunter shall rise and rule. Lament for he shall suffer. Rejoice for those days shall soon be over. He shall rule his people with an iron hand. His right arm shall be the deadly fangs of viper, full of terrible vengeance… He will create and nurture the Future World. The world shall call him an evil pirate. And his offspring shall praise and pamper him

At last, he shall die a totally disgraced King" said the enraged Spirit of the Sacred Oracle.

CHAPTER TWO

At the end of the spiritual consultation, Mr. Bingo departed a cursed and an angry man. He was so angry at himself that he decided to get even at the Great Spirit of the Oracle. After all, gods were there to protect those who served them. And the worshippers were there to follow, in wisdom, the footprints of the same gods.

It was a statement of fact, a fact so deeply rooted in native tradition and words of wisdom: "Whenever a god betrays a man, the man should hold such a god in contempt". Also, as the saying went in the land: "A mouse should not deliberately chew on a native doctor's medicine-bag. Lest the native doctor deliberately chew the baked head of the same mouse".

To Mr. Bingo, the Benevolent Spirit was more offensive than the offensive mouse. His initial plans were not only to kill the wicked witch who wanted to kill him, but also to kill the Python, the incarnate of the Oracle, and thus revert the curse, disgrace the

Oracle as a nuisance and rule the Kingdom as its Supreme Monarch. Firm as a rock, he was in his resolve.

Mr. Bingo had enough of life's hardships. When the opportunity became available to a legless dancer, to dance with active legs, he danced till the breaking point. If such a dancer were wise enough, he would definitely fight to retain the legs than just say "thank you" and let go. Mr. Bingo was that kind of man. He would neither return the active legs lent to him to dance, nor would he spare the lender who through oversight, stupidity, or something else, lent his useful legs to the needy one.

Mr. Bingo was, though blessed and cursed, a very offended man. He would neither put up with the curse of the Sacred Spirit of the Oracle, nor accept its verdict with regard to his newly found kingship in hardship in his royal domain, nor with its pronouncement on his future existence. And as far as Mr. Bingo was concerned, he would grab his own fate in his two hands, control it the way it would best serve his purpose. After all, a man who had found initial favor in the sight of the Great Spirit of the land, was not supposed to accept any contrary offer to the blessed arrangement.

A man who was determined to make his life count would not allow a fickle fate to use him as an escape-goat. And who among the peasants in a prosperous Kingdom would not accept an offer to become the King of his own land?

Mr. Bingo knew that the struggle would be a spiritual coup detat – A living hunter fighting the Royal Power of the departed souls. Apart from Python, the Supreme Incarnate, eagles, and cows, buffaloes and lions were the lesser, untouchable embodiments of the deities. And when the anger of the gods was upon a vengeful man, the gods better watch out, their annual sacrifices would likely be reduced…not only in quantity but also in quality.

And, of course, oftentimes the gods forget that, when a left-hand washed the right-hand, the right-hand would, in turn, wash the left-hand. Mr. Bingo knew this. He was, as the wise Sage often said: "A son of the soil". A man cheated by the gods when alive would also be cheated when his own spirit joined them. Therefore, he was determined to exploit to his best advantage, most of the whole situation.

King Bingo was tough and ruthless. For example, he became the Paramount King of a mighty empire whose lust for power, money and sex were known throughout the civilized world. Once he beheaded his first enemy, his own first wife, to set a special example for the masses – just to send his message across.

And after murdering his wife, his subjects hailed him "the most sincere King ever to rule the land".

Having gained the initial approval, he proceeded to pick fight with every other leader whose views and opinions were different from his.

Not many people among his subjects really knew how King Bingo gained access to the throne. Some said he overthrew the ex-King. However, the ex-King was not alive to voice out exactly what happened. The people were mesmerized to a confusing point. Ask anyone in the Kingdom: "What really happened?", he would give you one answer. Ask another the same question; he would give you an answer, an opposite at best.

The people and the entire Kingdom were tossed into a total chaos, to say the least. The people were so confused, mesmerized, and at a loss for answer that virtually, if not every soul in the land, every-one of them was able to invent an answer to explain away the fate of their former King.

Evidently, the answers they came up with were as many as the number of people in the land.

At the nick of time, one school of thought, mainly by a venerable Sage, said that King Bingo was voted in. but, the empire had no idea of democracy and its "one man one vote" system. It all happened, one glorious morning – that there was a long blast of trumpets; a chain of Imperial Warriors marching in a regal formation, women and children chanting and even elders joined them in their singing, dancing in the urban streets and market places, all in ceremonial welcome to a new King.

Everybody was happy that a redeemer was able to come at last. No one wanted to remember again anything good about any other King who ruled before King Bongo. As far as the people were concerned, King Bingo was "the Supreme Savior". And that alone did put every opposing view to rest – Buried forever.

Soon, "the Supreme Savior", King Bingo, became also known as "the Sword of the Oracle". Both his foes and friends knew that "the Sword of the Oracle" was holding back the hand of time. He discouraged any progress that was not attached to either any of his titles, or his real name.

Naturally, however, everyone was fearful, lest he end up in one of the royal gallows, constructed across the vast land; like the few enemies, mostly the gallows- birds, among them a gallow-humorist who dared to criticize him.

The youths would chant every morning in praise of the King. The elders would gnash their teeth in reminiscence of their grievances over the horrors they endured at the hands of the previous Kings – And they were encouraged to continue to do so. There was no doubt that everybody in the "New Empire" was having a great sigh of fake relief.

Allegiance to the new King, King Bingo was the first commandment of the land. King Bingo was to be truly obeyed, not criticized, by the subjects. The words of his mouth alone were powerful enough to make his most-potential critic shiver in his own hurt. After all, he would cite the fate of his first enemy, his own first wife, to remind his potential critics the danger ahead. And as if her case was not enough warning, he would add at every "Royal full-moon speech" to the Kingdom, the cases of the gallows-birds who were "disobedient to the Crown".

As the new King made his political in-road, he made more enemies abroad than he could handle. As mentioned earlier, he knew how to pick on neighboring Kingdoms. This alone was a mouthful of bite than a wise King could chew.

At home King Bingo ruled with an iron grip, and he drank every milk of praises by his people. But, in other kingdoms, his name was in a hot bathtub of political controversy; and his autocratic style was viewed with maximum contempt, to say the least.

As the King's critics looked forward to the King's fall, the King looked forward to a greater grip on his throne. For one thing, King Bingo knew: "To be great is to be feared", not necessarily loved. And through this fear one in power could equally claim the love.

King Bingo did just that. And his praises in the land bore the testimonies to the above. But the King's wife was not impressed. "It's a bold exercise in ignorance". The King's first wife dared to call it. And her acid tongue forced her to pay a price with her dear life.

When the King's wife was killed, her death earned the King a renewed dislike by his old enemies. Despite the hatred outside his Kingdom, the King felt the security of his position as his primary dream, while the hatred by distant Monarchs as of little consequence.

And although the neighboring Kingdoms hated him, they dared not challenge him. Because they feared his powerful warriors. Young men were recruited every full moon, trained in the arts of war, and armed to go in the warriors' ways. They were to defend their king, defend his Crown, defend their Kingdom, defend their sacred soil, and to defend themselves against their foes.

Despite all the hatred which the King and his people were aware of, one far-away Kingdom stood out as an exception – A lone empire, perhaps as powerful as his, maybe more powerful; but nonetheless an admirer and a friendly one – The lone Kingdom was Olarkwudo.

CHAPTER THREE

Kingsley Bingo was the first son of the King. He was the first child of his father by a second marriage. And his father, the King, wanted to give him the best royal training in the world – Thus preparing him for the throne.

Because of this dream, a plan so fervent in the King's heart, Kingsley was sent to Olarkwudo, the best Empire in the then world for the necessary training.

The King of Olarkwudo was not only a man of great means but also a friend of King Bingo. The two Kingdoms lived like twin brothers. They exchanged diplomatic missions and maintained a good inter-Kingdom relationship.

King Labata, for that was the name of King of Olarkwudo, was a brave man – A self-assured war hero who had little or no regard for people of lesser Kingdoms.

He valued a huge expanse of resources in that he could not do without it; he wielded a huge expanse of resources in that he could not do so without him. It was this mutual, special interests that bound the two Kings together not only in mutual trade but also in mutual respect.

When Kingsley came to Olarkwudo, he noticed that his physical feature, as curse rather than a blessing in disguise. The people in his home were simply square-headed.

The people, the Olarkwudoes, were so proud of themselves that anyone who was different from them, in any way, was considered an anathema.

Legend had it that the Olarkwudoes migrated from the third planet, Ilerum, to the galaxium, Earth, only to claim a part of it as their rightful inheritance. The original natives of the land, the Jikikans, were slaughtered by the murderous imperialists from the third planet. And their dead bodies fed to the dogs and the special vultures that came with them. Few Jikikans survived. And the very few Jikikans who survived the onslaught became endangered species. The people have endured this status till this day.

Eventually the survivors could not pay in specie, because such a move would have marked the end of their race.

King Bingo learnt about this; but, this event, if ever it did occur, occurred over a thousand millennium ago. The remnants of Jikika Kingdom who knew themselves as the true owners of the land, knew they could no longer fight nor re-conquer their ancient conquerors.

One could easily see the same head shape come true – The Jikikans, were triangular headed – As such, were regarded as inferiors.

Kingsley saw a few of them shunned by the majority of the Olarkwudoes. But he chose to be-friend them. His friendship with the few outcasts yielded him a special lesson, a history in suffering, enslavement and human's inhumanity to human.

The Old Spirit, in whom the Jikikans prided themselves, sold them free of charge into the hands of foul fate. They were reduced to the point that they had to beg for survival. Indeed, the once proud people lost their pride. To dream of enjoying the minimum standard of living ably despised by the poorest conquerors, the Olarkwudoes, the true owners of the land became the rejected beggars, who begged without shame.

With the passage of time, the Olarkwudoes re-named the "Old Spirit", the "Great Spirit" and worshipped him. This deity was a very angry and a very benevolent one.

Originally, the Olarkwudoes came in with their own unique fate and their own Powerful Deity. And in reminiscence of their favorable voyage, through time and space, round buildings were designed, constructed, and built as high temples for their own Powerful Deity.

At first, the Jikikans were pleasantly amused, even surprised as they tasted the simple ways of the seemingly weak voyagers. The Jikikans worshipped with pomp and gallantry Dancing was pretty common during their worship ritual. This they did with unbounding energy. in their religious rituals. For them, the quest to worship any deity knew no limitation.

In fact, everything that breathed the air-of-life, in the land, was worthy to be worshipped by the people, in their seasons, in a very special way – Indeed, the trees, for example, were worshipped as gods that grew on the land. And mere animals, for instance, were truly and constantly worshipped as gods that walked on the land. And variety of fishes, in the world of water, were worshipped as gods that swam in the water.

Large and small birds were worshipped, by the people, as gods that flew in the sky. Also snails, rodents and worms were equally worshipped as true gods that dwelt in the soil.

True, the Jikikans were true worshippers. To them, to be human was to be a worshipper. And they made a god of every far lesser organism than they.

Every creature had its own station as a living god. The Jikikans knew this, honored it as their legacy – A legacy passed down unto them by their worshipping forebears. This was their way before the conquest – A conquest that displaced their tradition and placed them not only in a subservient position, but worse, in an endangered list.

No one knew how long they had been worshipping before the invaders, the Olarkwudoes came. But an age-old legend had it that the Jikikans had been a Kingdom of worshippers as far long as their living memory could fathom. In short, to worship was a part of their culture passed on from one generation to another.

Kingsley could not help but feel for them – He felt for their lost glory, their shrieked identity and their hopeless existence. His feelings gave way to a spirit of compassion. He began to give them some gifts. He gave away some of his personal wealth to a few of the wretched lot, only to find out that the more he was willing to give, the greater the number of the wretched Jikikans that thronged around him.

He would not drive them away, because they clamored to him as their living hope. Babies crying in the hands of their mothers were stretching out their hands towards him – Women in their late years were wailing for his assistance.

The half-naked men once tortured with procustes by the invaders, now found some strength to tramp on their weaker ones… in their drive to get closer to him. Kingsley found himself thronged and trapped for hours on end whenever he paid a visit to the chained forest reserve, exclusively for the unfortunate Jikikans.

There was no doubt that Prince Kingsley was courting inter-Kingdom trouble by helping those who could not help themselves.

"A lone rebel from a distant land has been methodically organizing a social unrest", the King's vinous adviser, Sokoya Aligaro, remarked. The King was untouched by his remark because the adviser was drunk when those words slipped out of his mouth.

As time passed by, Kingsley became more and more involved in the lives of the unfortunate ones. Their dying rituals became his obsession; initiating along the way a revival of interest in the dying traditions. And he became more incensed by the plights of the unfortunate ones. It was this complete change of heart that turned the ire of the King.

Twice King Labata saw him lead a protest mission for Jikika remnants. Those, to his own palace. Cheerfully he honored a request to award every Jikikan a semblance of identity in the Kingdom.

Just like Prince Kingsley's father, astute, crafty and dubious, King Labata was able to conceal his true feeling in the presence of a multitude of people. Deep inside, King Labata did not like the idea. But Kingsley got his way with him. He honored the protest demand out of respect for Kingsley's father, his special friend.

The Jikikans knew that the Old Spirit remembered them. There were a few among them who were entertaining hope that one day their total deliverance would come through the hands of their new god, Kingsley, their god in human form.

The hope of the Jikikans began to be on the rise as they saw its symbol daily in the person of their new god from a distant land. Kingsley continued to increase his activities for them, thereby incurring increased secret displeasure of the King.

Events were turning the tide. Fate which made a god of a royal one was making him a rebel in the others' sight. Of course, rumor began to spread that King Labata was preparing to send a special emissary to ask King Bingo a few words:

"Kindly recall your son home". But it turned out the conservative King preferred to leave the reckless prince alone – Just for a reason: To avoid his father's unpleasant reaction.

CHAPTER FOUR

A year later, the King and the King's men left the palace for a hunting expedition. The King, mounted on a royal elephant had his spears, bows and poisoned arrows ready to hunt.

It was the King's annual custom to go on a week-long hunting safari. This event was a neatly designed concept to give the crown an exotic deviation from the all-year-long royal activities.

There were more than two hundred armed men in the hunting entourage. A hundred men went before him in the royal forest. These men should shout, shake the trees, and make all sorts of noises, thus, arouse the hidden beasts from their hiding places. The other people were following behind the king in the process. They were also shouting and harassing the wild beasts, arousing, and revealing and scaring the forest dwellers to death. And the King was having a hay-day. He could not leave well enough alone. At least, this day.

Before the middle of the day, the King killed more animals than he had in any other safari expedition. By noon that same day, he killed more than a dozen beasts before he even reached the middle of his forest.

As said, he was enjoying it. Among his kills were an antelope, three leopards, two buffaloes, two tigers and some wild pigs. The King had not even had his breakfast. To be sure, his mind was away from it, being taken away by the all-more-important hunting safari…Such was the joy of the day.

Suddenly, the King's men aroused a female lion from its hiding place. Quick as a trained hunter, the King raised his spear and threw it at the fleeing beast. The spear's poisoned blade caught the helpless animal at the back. Within a moment, its sharp blade pierced through the lioness' vertebral column. With a feeble groan the beast fell and died.

But a few steps away from the King, was a male lion, obviously the husband of the slain beast. When the couple heard the noise, they were so startled that while the confused female lion ran out from their den, her husband climbed a low nearby tree in wait for the eventuality.

The beast saw the King kill its wife and resolved to take its revenge. The animal was quiet on the low tree's branch, concealed by the low tree's leaves, angry at the man who killed its wife, and ready to spring at him in revenge.

And hardly the King dismounted from the royal elephant, all in total triumph, to be the first person to touch his kill, when the angry lion sprang on him. He died on the spot, instantly, right on top of the beast he just slew.

Alarmed at what happened, some of the King's guards rushed to his rescue. The lion saw the armed men approach, took off on a high speed.

When they touched the King, the King was already lifeless. And when some of the King's men tried to pursue the lion, the lion was nowhere to be found.

When the news of King Labata's violent death reached the chained forest, the Jikikans rejoiced. Some of the native Jikikans chanted, danced and made merry.

The natives erected not only an altar, but also molded a stature of a lion in the middle of the forest. As far as the natives saw him, King Labata was the "abominable vulture". They saw his painful death as a reward, by the Old Spirit, on the man at the fullness of time. More so, another sign of their future deliverance.

King Warrior Batuque considered himself in a sea of fire when he was fighting in his last battlefield. He was a man who was trained to fight. He had known wars all his life. He had seen battles, and he had taken a few heads of his foes from battlefields back home in his youthful days.

Indeed, it was his heroic performance in a strange war with Kitoquois tribe that brought him closer to the crown when he was but a youth.

When Batuque became a new King, no one doubted he would. He was the favorite of his people, of the gods, and even of the Great Spirit. A few of his men died in battles when he led them…, Moreso, rather nil in the battles with the tribe of Kitoquois.

In fact, it was reported that any warrior fighting under the command of warrior Batuque was under the wings of the Great Spirit. Such was the man who was tapped, after several prophecies by the medicine men, and revelations through the venerable astrologers and necromancers, to lead his people as "The Leader Warrior: The Chosen King".

King Batuque knew how much the natives hated the last King. And he was determined, not only to erase his legacy, but more beautifully, not to follow in his ways.

One of the earliest things King Batuque did when he became the King was to recognize the natives and their gods. For example, he gave the natives a total assimilation. It was an edict that won him the hearts of his people, the hearts of the natives, the heart of the Old Spirit, now Great Spirit, and the heart of Prince Kingsley.

King Warrior Batuque considered himself as a brave king; indeed, he was. He knew himself as lord of the battles; indeed, by dint of action, he proved it to his people. This time, things were changing so rapidly beyond his royal control. For example, the hand of fate, which was once passionate in his favor, was turning against him. For the first time in his life, he began to fear, not only for his people, his kingdom, his family and even for his own dear life.

"Fate has betrayed us; but there is no going back". he said to his men. As a man of war, he knew nothing could deter a warrior under the pure flames of passion.

"Why are you saying all these things, your majesty?" one of the King's advisers asked, bowing in the process.

"Because in the olden days the King's presence in the battle was a clear sign of his commitment to his war. But I am fighting to defend our walls. Another King whose face I have never seen has so low a regard for me that he does not come to the battle to fight me, man to man. Rather, he sends his men, dangerous as they are, to kill our men, capture our warriors, take our women, daughters and young ones as captives.

We fight people whose language we do not know. They have no regard for the rules of war. I don't know what they have in mind---They kill everything within their reach. They are the locust's warriors of our time.

They ride on the back of animal, and their animals help them with the fight. When their weapons did not kill our men, their animals kick our men, killing some, at times, wounding them. You all have seen it. It is a dangerous war". Then the King stopped.

The adviser bowed again in total allegiance. The King in turn touched his head with his golden sword. Then the man lifted his face.

"May the King rule forever" the man said.

"Your words are kind. May the Great Spirit hear" the King responded. The way the King said those words; there was a subtle clue of deep reservation.

As a King, he was not supposed to show off any emotion that would reflect him as a coward before his own fighting men. All his war advisers knew this protocol and did everything at their disposal to build the King's confidence.

It was before the reign of King Warrior Batuque when Prince Kingsley came here to receive his royal training in the King's court. There were no such things as "schools" in those days, such in this kingdom; those, at least. Learning was a set of practical experience. Here were the rituals, the practical customs and traditions passed over trough practice and words of mouth.

Annually, the people would offer some crop sacrifices in the holy forest, thus, appeasing not only the demi-gods, but the Great

Spirit as well. They would plead with the gods for bountiful harvest and perpetual protection.

Prince Kingsley was greatly impressed because in many ways, their customs and the traditions of his own people had great similarities. Their marriage customs were similar, safe a few variations in the stages of marriage.

The people had a blind trust in the King's decisions, just like they did in his home. They were friendly to strangers because the new King, King Batuque, saw to it as a part of the native heritage. It was fast and amazing how the invaders adapted to the natives' ways. In fairness to the new trend, Kingsley began to find himself in a new home, not less his former home, away from home.

With the passage of time, Prince Kingsley decided to pay the new King in kind. It became more and more evident that Prince Kingsley liked it there. Every new moon King Warrior Batuque sent some of his emissaries to King Bingo to give a progress report on his son. This special caring gave Prince Kingsley a special sense of belonging. In turn, King Bingo loaded the emissaries with royal gifts of spices, dried snake skins, plums, nectarines, onions and ginger leaves.

Once King Bingo sent, among his usual gifts, a beautiful bride. This damsel was one of the most beautiful virgins obtainable from his kingdom. King warrior Batuque was so touched by the offer that he rewarded King Bingo by adopting Prince Kingsley into his inner circle – The most-trusted King's advisers.

From these men, seven in number, would be nominated by oracle a new King when the King was gone. Warrior Batuque was an eminent member of this group when King Labata ruled the land.

Warrior Batuque doubled as a lone warrior in the King's inner circle when King Labata ruled the land. Since his death, hence the elevation of warrior Batuque to the throne, the members of the inner circle operated by an aggregate of six. Now with the nomination of Prince Kingsley into the group, the requisite number of people for the King's inner circle became complete.

It was a special honor; first of its kind, upon once a total stranger, a radical one so, in the land. The news of this bestowment flashed home to King Bingo's ears. And he was greatly satisfied.

"My son will be a King either at home or abroad", King Bingo said radiating with joy.

From then on, more than ever, that with passage of time, Prince Kingsley saw himself more, no longer a Prince, but a dual Prince with two kingdoms, potentially at his back and call. He acted accordingly. And his love for the people showed.

He initiated a rapid exchange in trade, information, and marriage. And the two kings approved. Then the two kingdoms applied. He saw his reputation soar. He was happy about it.

Prince Kingsley was not satisfied. His human tendency to indefinite and insatiable desire multiplied and soared. He saw himself as an asset of two kingdoms…the useful Crown Prince of the two people and was ready to capitalize and communize on it. He organized the able young men who were about to get married.

In addition, he made some receptive arrangements with unmarried virgins in each of the two kingdoms. At last, he got the unmarried people to get together in some romantic, social settings. And the results were numerous inter-kingdom marriages.

These moves alone brought the two kingdoms much closer. The Kingdoms and the people knew the brain behind all these. The name Kingsley became a talk of the day. The title Prince Kingsley became synonymous with "unity among two kingdoms".

Kingsley became the favorite member of the King's Inner-Circle; often-times the King would not only confide in him, but seek his words of wisdom on issues of royal importance.

Time without number, King warrior Batuque told Prince Kingsley about his heroic exploits during his youthful days. Oftentimes, the King added some special colorings, and some dramatic touches to some of the stories he told Prince Kingsley as he re-told the same stories over and over again.

Prince Kingsley knew that the King loved him, and he was willing to retain his love. Obviously, Kingsley was greatly impressed. More so, to be under the wings of a man who had ably and in great measure, proven himself a man, a warrior, and a Great King.

When King Warrior Batuque received the initial threat from the Pirate Dukedom, Prince Kingsley was so infuriated that he volunteered to lead the King's warriors in the first battle engagement. But the King refused. Protocol, and indeed, the custom and tradition of the people would not endorse such. Despite all things, Prince Kingsley was primarily a future King of a foreign land.

Prudence alone was a strong enough voice of caution, primarily to caution King Warrior Batuque to keep his most precious guest away from harm's way.

CHAPTER FIVE

In the King's Royal Court were the King's men discussing the invasions of the Royal Kingdom by many foreign mind-twisting philosophies and very invasive, psychological sects, known as religions. Christianity and Islam, for example, came in because of what Prince Kingsley did. For example, one must remember the marriages and other contacts the two kingdoms made. That the people from the two kingdoms did go with them, all the way, along the way, was a fact and the living legacy of the great human exchange between the two Great Kingdoms that found reason to bond in mutual friendship.

Suffice to note, however, that there were many rapid cross-fertilization of ideas, value systems, rituals, and what have you…Among them, major and minor religions. These religions, as the Royal Queen of the land came to realize, were not only physically invasive but also psychologically and even spiritually enslaving. And the Spiritual Founders of the invasive sects led the charge without being seen while they invaded the New Kingdom.

Twelve different ideals invaded the land, spiritually. And ten of these ideals were pretty invasive religions. For example, that people die and came back as either trees, rats, ants, worms, snakes, cows, dogs, or even lame and dirty pigs was the wonder-making idea that came from Hindu religion into the land. And Islam came from Saudi Arabia into the land with swords and bloodbath.

Hindu, though so wonderful, was the oldest religion that the mind of a man ever invented. And the Wise Guru who came up with the idea was a man of India, Shinto, as a sect, was a collection of Japanese customs and practical traditions. And Taoism and Confucius teachings were mere Chinese philosophies.

Sikhism and Jainism came from India. And Bahai and Zoroastrianism had their origin in the Kingdom of Persia. Christianity, though extremely invasive, and Judaism, so insular, came from the nation of Israel.

Some of these religions came into the New Kingdom with great ideas. And some of them came with deadly ones. There were some whose doctrines were either morally uplifting, morally retrogressive, or morally reprehensible. Indeed, these ideals were the outgrowths of great thinkers, the Epic Gurus of their esteemed enclaves. They were mainly the Religions of the Orients.

The core doctrines of the Oriental sects differed from one another. A sect, called Buddhism, for example, did not believe in a Supreme Deity who lived somewhere in the vast, open sky.

Christian sect and Islamic faith, however, believed in the Supreme One. But Muslims believed that their singular 'Allah' was so bloody that violence and bloodbath were the only roads that could enable them spread His message to the whole world.

Christians, however, were of the unique opinion that love and mercy would win souls. Also, they were of the opinion that their Supreme One were Three Unique Deities in One Supreme Being. Worship of the ancestors, by anyone in the land was viewed as 'mere paganism' by both Christians and Muslims.

Animism was not a new thing, because the people knew it, and they were used to it. Christianity, on the other hand, became the nagging bell in their hearts – it condemned everything they held supreme as paganism.

On the other hand, the Islam made some rooms for certain provisions. Acceptance of the enlightened ones, as the beacons of light of the society, was a case in point.

The women of the two great religions were not really allowed to open their mouths, by the elites of the two great religions. These same marginalized women were only mere numbers in the man-made congregations. Indeed, these poor women were mere objects to be seen in the religious meetings, and not to be heard. To this end, many ridiculous man-made laws, codes and dogmas were put in place, so as to keep the women pretty subservient to the fewer men in all the religious congregations.

The invasive religion, known as Christianity, was constantly proclaimed as the "good news". Many people, mostly men, turned in great number, to it. But some women, in the kingdom, saw it in a different light. And so many of the enlightened women were so skeptical.

"A true 'good news' does not gag you" the King's wife protested.

At first, when she heard the "good news", she flew into a clear rage. All the armors of her natural suspicious were raised to their highest state of alertness. Now with the defenses of the new religious posturing and ready to gag her and other women, she had one option: To answer a bonfire with an inferno for the public to witness.

On the Queen's part, there was no need to turn back. Resolved and determined, she attacked both Christianity and Islamic faith as "dubious religions".

Indeed, as the saying went in the land: "A wise man would not argue with a woman, for its always obvious, she would win the argument". However, these religious leaders were a set of different men with some sets of different topics; these sets of different men chose to walk on the sacred ground, many a case in an issue where otherwise men, mostly the Sacred Sages in the land, had chosen to avoid.

The woman was on the defensive. She knew her rights to voice out her resentments. The preachers, Christians and Muslims, were determined to put her, in what they presumed to be her rightful place, as far as their religions were concerned.

"Whosoever willeth, mayest come" said a wise Pastor of one of the two invading religious faiths.

Right after the discussion in the King's Court, Prince Kingsley paid his usual courtesy visit to the Royal Queen. Madam Queen Olakugio was a beautiful, middle-aged woman. She was not only royally tough, but also maternally gracious; tense at times, but beautifully gracious, too. She was a woman of dual disposition. Those who hardly knew her, the viewers at a distance, thought she was a wicked witch. However, those who knew better, those who had an intimate relationship with her, held her with a special adoration.

Prince Kingsley knew her feelings towards the two new religions. And as such, he was not in the best of disposition to make bones about them. After all, there was a greater royal duty at the calling. For instance, the threat by the Pirate Duke Mento Mino, to the Prince, was a mountain compared to the mere mole hills, known as the two invasive religions.

Hardly had Prince Kingsley greeted her when she bared up her mind:

"Their own conscience, together with the Spirit of the Lord bear witness that they are children of abomination" said the angry Queen. She was very angry because an irate Christian Preacher insulted her. In all her life, no one had insulted her the way the Christian Preacher did insult her.

In her bid to reason with him, the young, self-righteous Preacher told her in no unapologetic terms:

"Unless you repent, you shall, all likewise perish" said the rude Preacher. His words did hurt her. His stinging words were so corrosive in an acidic proportion.

CHAPTER FIVE (B)

Prince Kingsley heard about the verbal fight she had with that insolent Preacher. Precisely, he learnt about it during the royal meeting in the King's Court.

Kingsley knew that the easiest way to appease an offended woman was to take side with her…That, at least, till her high temper calmed down. With tact and wisdom, he queried her in a way that showed her that he was right there on her side.

"What Lord, the Great Spirit?" Prince Kingsley asked the Queen.

"You are damn right. Their souls, I decree, to hell, be damned" the Queen declared with an answer.

"That is a hard verdict, though," Kingsley added a note of reconciliation. The Prince and the Queen liked each other. And they knew it. Oftentimes, they came to each other's defense.

"Yes, they deserve it" the Queen stood firm. She was not ready to change her mind, her decree, and her position..

"It's unfortunate you cannot even trust any Christian in this world". Kingsley added, signaling in passing, his total lack of trust in the ways some Christian leaders behaved.

The Queen glowed in triumph, knowing her trusted ally was totally on her side.

"Not just Christians, Muslims too" she went ahead and condemned the Muslims, too.

"I think Muslims are more honest," The Prince said with a chord of slight disagreement, but the woman was ready for that.

"You really don't know them," the Queen responded. As if that alone was not enough to dispel his doubt, she added a few more words to convince him: "Let me tell you a story. Muslims are not supposed to drink wine, right?"

"That's correct, and they don't".

"That's wrong".

"Have you seen any, eh?" asked Prince Kingsley.

"Yes, the hypocritical ones" answered the Queen.

"How can that be?" Prince Kingsley asked in a way, as of one in quest for more informative answers.

"Listen, you, now. Are you?"

"Yes, I am".

"Use your smallest fingers to clean your ears carefully before I say another word" said the Queen, teasing Prince Kingsley in the process.

"Ah, please don't do me that. Your Royal Majesty, kindly don't treat me like a mere child. I am neither deaf nor dumb." responded Prince Kingsley with feigned facial protest.

"That's fine. Better you are listening" said the Queen.

"Please, go ahead, Your Majesty". Kingsley continued to give her his go ahead nudge.

"They go to the mosques on Fridays to worship their Allah. Is that not true?"

"Yes, that's very correct." answered Prince Kingsley.

"Also, they carry some water in some kettles to their Mosques. Not so?" asked the Queen, like someone who knew the Moslems; religious custom very well.

"Yes, in their kettles, yes, to wash their feet, their religious ritual, yes".

"Some of them do not carry water in those kettles" said the Queen.

"What then do they carry if not water?" Prince Kingsley asked the Queen, in an air of total surprise.

"Tombo" answered the Queen.

"You are kidding, Your Majesty. Muslims are not supposed to carry wine to their places of worship. Do they?" shouted Prince Kingsley.

"But they do so; they do not only carry their strong tombo into the Mosques, they drink it, and drink it on their way home" the Queen replied in a subdued way. Her facial expression telling the message that she had a case against them.

"That's silly, awful and foolish" said Prince Kingsley.

"Yes, as silly, awful and as foolish as the behaviors of the so-called Christian Ministers of the gospel who preach, 'Thou shalt not commit adultery', yet, they do it with reckless impunity" said the angry Queen.

"It is not only adultery though. They steal, they tell lies. They covet. They are envious. They defend racism. And they practice against everything they are supposed to stand for its cause" Prince Kingsley added his own list of indictments.

"Pity them. Their lots are sealed" said the tough Queen, as she began to relax a bit. After all, she was a woman. She tempted to switch roles. Her feminine instinct, full of compassion, took over. The Prince, however, brought her back to the issue at stake…the very topic under discussion:

"Your Majesty, they deserve no pity, not even from their own heavenly God" said Prince Kingsley.

"Wow, son, did you just say that?" asked the Queen.

"Your Majesty, I hate them more than you do. I really do, because they are nothing less than perfect bunch of unrepentant hypocrites" said Prince Kingsley.

"That young man was so full of himself that he felt that he was more righteous than his own God in the empty sky" said the Queen.

"Your Majesty, should that useless Pastor come here to preach to you again, do me a favor by asking him a very simple question" said Prince Kingsley.

"Yes, my dear, what should I ask him?" asked the Queen.

"Please ask him: Why are you here to lynch me psychologically the way those that sent you here lynched the Son of your God physically? Yes, Your Majesty, once you received him with that soul-searching question, it would definitely dawn on him that he and those that sent him are nothing but common, if not bloody, dishonest bunch" answered Prince Kingsley.

"I knew it. Yes, I do that those who called themselves the Messengers of Good News were nothing but Vectors of Bad News. They are hypocrites. I knew they were hiding ugly something in their dirty closet" said the Queen with voice of triumph.

"Yes, Your Majesty, such people are pretty dishonest group" said Prince Kingsley.

"Thank you my dear. I shall store that vital question on the clean table of my mind. And whenever that fool or his fellow fools come here, to poison the mind of anyone in this palace with their evil news, I shall chase them away with that same vital question" said the Queen.

"Thanks Your Majesty; it's really a great pleasure" said the Prince.

"Yes, I shall do it, with speedy exactitude, whenever I see any of them anywhere, in this Royal Compound" said the Queen.

"I know, you can, Your Majesty. A soul-searching question is a great weapon. Once you hit them with that question, it will knock them out the way a boxer-champion knocks down his opponent in a boxing ring" said Prince Kingsley.

CHAPTER FIVE (C)

They came from the land where a damsel changed into a cunning lad. Then, the cunning lad morphed into a very ambitious young man. And then, the ambitious young man became a drug lord. As he became rich by narcotics, he joined the politics of the Caliphate of Corruption.

He bribed his way to the hearts of the King-Makers of the Paradise of Corruption. Boatloads of bribes paved the way for him. As such, the damsel who became a lad eventually landed the top job of the Island that was once colonized by the armed bandits in red-coats.

Indeed, they came from the human Zoo where a Fula-man became a no-nonsense Dictator. A corrupt Dictator who emerged from nowhere to mow down some minor corruption, he built monumental mountains of corruption that made the corrupt Tower of Babel look like a mere toy.

When he died in the Land of Red-coats, known as London, some corrupt men flew his body over to Saudi Arabia where it was buried in a mere shallow grave. A man from a born-to-rule tribe, his kinsmen quickly brought in a fake Dictator to continue to rule for the decaying corpse in a shallow grave.

The Kingdom of Kidnappers rose, dwindled and died. All these things happened to the evil Kingdom because the born-to-rule tribe chose to enslave the land and her people with iron fists. For example, corruption was the virus that killed the Caliphate from within. Yes, stings of corruption killed the nation.

When the nation began to die, the children of the nation began to scatter all over the world. These young ones from the Eminent Caliphate of Corruption were ants of knowledge. Quickly, they embraced the rich knowledge of their new environments.

The new environments offered them the wealth of opportunities to work, learn and earn their keep without the dew, rain, or the sunlight of corruption. Many of them made it, big time, in the New Kingdom where the Corruption of the Caliphate was a distant memory. They met so many alpha females in the New Land. These were girls and women who were so talented that they could easily perform any task faster, better, and even more proficient than boys and men. Among them were the supreme control freaks and ultra-drum-majors with extra-ordinary skills.

These girls and women were so endowed that they could do anything that boys and men could do, even twice better than their male counterparts. The changes in mind and perception that the ants of enlightenment went through were the baptisms of fiery renaissance. They changed inside out. Memories of the Rulers of the Zoo were always fresh in their minds. For example, when the born-to-rule Fula-men wanted to steal the lands from the peaceful owners of the lands, they went about it on the back of horses, even with swords of war.

They deceived the victims with their violent Islam, while at the same time they grabbed the lands from the victims. The ants of enlightenment remembered all the things that the born-to-rule Fula-men did in their land of birth. Even as they did, they witnessed a world of distinction in the New Land. For example, they saw the ponds of irrational hate and irrational fear. They saw Sikh-o-phobia in action. They saw Buddhi-o-phobia in action. They saw Hindu-phobia in action.

Also, they saw hatred against Jews, hatred against Arabs, hatred against Blacks, and even hatred against anyone with accent, anyone with physical deformity, and anyone who looked different from the invaders who conquered and took over the land from the natives.

"We Black People worship Allah more than any other human race. Sadly, we are also the least blessed by the same Allah" said a terribly disappointed Mumu Muslim man.

"Why so? Does that mean that your Allah hates those who worship him the most?" asked an Iberibe man.

"I do not know" answered the Mumu Muslim man.

"You do not know?" asked the Iberiberized Christian man.

"Yoo-wah. I do not know"

"You should know why your Allah chose to bless you less, since you are a regular worshipper; at the same time, he chose to bless, much more, the irregular worshippers. Honestly, something is off the mark. If I were you, I would not only demand to be blessed, should my Allah refuse to bless me, then, I shall refuse to worship him till he repents and begins to bless me with uncommon boatloads of blessings" said the Iberiberized man with a grain of common sense in his baptized mind.

CHAPTER SIX

Far away from the ancient Kingdom was a Dukedom ruled by powerful pirates. It was reported that crooks and other worst of criminals were the Royal Lions and Princely Tigers that were having their hay-day.

Kingsley's father, King Bingo, the Paramount King of the Kingdom, learnt about that Dukedom and feared for the worst. He knew that some of those pirating hoodlums could easily send their spies and trouble-makers to other kingdoms, just to create troubles for them.

He had fought a couple of wars, victorious in each, before his son, Kingsley came of age. But this time, he did not want to be involved in another war. He knew that two kingdoms could easily pick fight with each other---that and when their belief and practices were at variance with each other.

Because of these, he decided to take precaution. Although his kingdom was secure with superior warriors, wise men, wide and tall rock-solid walls, and advanced civilization, he knew internal troubles would be much more difficult to manage than a fight coming across the borders. This, of course, was one of the main reasons, internal security as said, that made the King to send the Prince to a peace-loving Kingdom, to learn other ways of running, rather, of ruling a great and vast Kingdom.

He knew that knowledge would forever be the embodiment of power. That those who despise it would forever live in regrets. Therefore, being a man of vision, he foresaw the need for his own son to avail himself of all the best knowledge on earth that he could garner from the best minds in a distant land.

No kingdom, as the King reasoned, could provide such a sound knowledge than a kingdom rich in culture, sound in wisdom, backed by solid and reputable growth for a thousand rains of undisturbed peace, and civilization.

This was an ancient Kingdom, far away from the harm's way. Its borders were inviting, open and blessed. Besides, the members of the ancient Kingdom in question were known for their broad and open-mindedness. Some oral messages in those days told tales of diamonds and gold being used in decorating their doorposts.

Majority of the people, just like the natives in King Bingo's Kingdom, heard the sweet news of this Kingdom of Olarkwudo. It was also because of this great rumor that excited the Pirates'

Dukedom and its leadership to establish a "trade contract" with the ancient Kingdom far away.

A few days prior to his son's scheduled departure, King Bingo hastily made a firm decision to lick his vomit. For example, twice he burnt the forest of the Oracle…just to show his people that the Oracle was a nuisance.

It was "a spiritual disgrace of the highest order" which did not only earn him displeasure of the necromancers, but a displeasure which claimed their lives as well. This time, around, the King sought to divine through the remnants of the medicine-men what fate had in store for his son.

As the King approached the first medicine-man early in the morning, after the first cockcrow, lo, and behold, there came forth some terrible utterances. The mourning voices of the dead souls interrupting one another saying:

The first voice:	Woe betide those who think that evil is right and that wrong is good.
Another voice:	"I am the Lord of this jungle, you swine".
The first voice again:	"Woe betide those who cheat the orphan, homeless and deprive the illegal aliens in their midst".
Yet another voice:	"What do you mean by that?"

The most vocal first voice once again: "Yes, woes forever abide and betide those who adhere to the evil idea that salvation is by color".

Again, the King of the people forgot the wise admonition of his own people that,

"He who eats with the spirits from the same bowl must use a long and sharply-pointed metallic fork".

Yes, King Bingo miscalculated again, and thought the spirits of these dead were still his subjects. He thought he could say anything, anyhow in their spiritual presence.

"What are they talking about?" the King asked the medicine-man, as the two men sat, divining, before the Holy Shrine of the Oracle.

"Your head" a female voice of a departed soul insulted him.

King Bingo was infuriated by her insult. Without finding an answer to his mission, he stood up, speechless, took off and left.

The woman, the old spirit, known then as "the Green Dragon", was a vector of a grave disease, called tuberculosis. She died of the same disease. And she had been passing her grave disease to those she disliked, especially when her living enemies came to consult for answers at the Oracle of the medicine man.

King Bingo hardly knew he would get it when the woman insulted him. She had passed on her terrible sickness to more than four score and ten people. And more than one score and ten of those she gave it had joined her in the Spirits' world.

She saw to it that those she successfully gave her disease never recovered from it. Having lived a slave in the human world, and now a giant in the other world, she was able to confuse any medicine man who tried to cure those she inflicted with the sickness. That alone was her way of taking revenge on those who treated her and her own race badly before she died.

It was an age of servitude. The age one ethnic race was subdued and exploited.

People were frustrated, especially those who were exploited. The rich people in the kingdom were only the members of the King's tribe. And no one would doubt the sacred truth in the Priest's prophecy: A truth so self-evident in action and in the way the people lived.

"There is no miscegenation in the land because the gods of the other people do love them more".

The lords in the lands of the Spirits held a meeting and decreed it. Obviously, their agreement found an expression in the sad prophecy. At the initial point, however, majority of those who were later suppressed thought it a bluff of the departed souls.

Later, the sad truth came home to roost. This was ten thousand years ago, a solar millennium before King Bingo was even born.

At that time, the people laughed heartily at the voice of the omen. Those who knew the Chief Priest in that event, very well, in those days narrated that he had a husky voice and, at times, his words could not be audible enough for those around him to hear.

Since the sad prophecy came to its fulfillment, the entire kingdom had not remained the same. Killing of the unloved, and every less loved ethnic race member, became an issue below the law.

The powers-that-were, really were rather not ready nor willing to make any bones about the grievances, especially when they were many an issue brought forward by the unfortunate race.

"Oh, those people again", was a dismissing phrase about them. The King himself was the least interested, talk-less his henchmen who more than many times advocated for the eradication of the inferior race.

It was under this condition that King Bingo ruled. Also, it was also under this condition that the Paramount Ruler decided to perpetuate his dynasty. But his son, Prince Kingsley, was a different man. His experience among the natives, under the rule of King Labata, had already given him a better understanding of his father's land.

CHAPTER SEVEN

There was a general agreement among the King's cabinet: 'If the war did not go well, exonerate the King''. After all, they were there to protect the image and interest of the King.

It was the year Prince Kingsley was born. The year the King routed all his enemies, left and right, north and south, in the first war after he became the King. The King's warriors were surprised at the rate of their victories in all the battles.

"Kome, let me kill you" was the trench-cleaning slogan that each and every victorious King's warrior used as they pursued their helpless enemy warriors, killing them along the way.

The King then was at the height of his glory, early as it was. True, the King later approved each expedition and claimed its glory. That was then, many years ago.

By this time, though the King had to face a different kind of enemy. As things would turn out, it would be a challenge of his life. His son was in a friendly, but a foreign land.

Mento Mino heard that Kingsley was seriously against his intent to invade. Therefore, he decided to seize him from existence. He knew that the stakes were high. If he failed, the news would leak, and his Pirate Dukedom would have to fight two strong Kingdoms at multiple war fronts, at the same time. It was a thing he did not want to happen; at least, for the time being.

Being a man of uncanny strategies, he decided to grab every desirable kingdom, one at a time. He knew, through strength there was might. And by might, right. He decided to recuperate… Just like a python would take a period of rest after swallowing another snake…By so doing, gain a new strength for a new conquest.

Duke Mino was not lacking in effective ideas on what to do. After all, he was the Pirate Duke, a notorious Pirate Duke whose reputation was dreaded not just by his friends…More so by those who were unfortunate enough to have felt the stings of his terrible hands.

One of his plots was to kidnap Kingsley in a way that would leave no trace. By so doing, his paternal Kingdom and his adoptive Kingdom would have not only a great misunderstanding, but a fight as well. That would weaken the two kingdoms. Then, his Pirate Dukedom would go in as a hunting hawk would go to a burnt farmland and pick up the kills.

It was a delicate plot that needed a careful execution. In the heat of the plot Duke Mento Mino decided that the surest way to do it was to send some specially trained warriors to the Kingdom of the Olarkwudos and get it done. First, they would go in disguise as angels of friendship.

Their mission would keep them for many moons, perhaps two winters in the foreign land. They would be-friend Kingsley, socialize with him, learn his ways until he became comfortable enough with them as to trust them. And at last, at the wee moment, they must capture him alive without bodily harm and transport him to the Pirate Dukedom. They had to, following the Duke's special mandate: leave no clue as to his where about.

Duke Mento Mino was a subtle man. So subtle that he would exercise an everlasting patience to get whatever he wanted. No matter what that was. For sure, he knew, to kidnap Prince Kingsley, rather, to get him out of the way, he would have to keep his nose "patiently on the grindstone" so to speak.

Common sense as ever, did dictate wisdom. If one man were right at a point, this did not imply that he would be right in all things.

There are times when one should recognize and appreciate what others are doing for or against on their many a behalf. There are also a set of common sense. Common sense in that sacrifice is a seed of things at hand, seed of things unseen, and seed of things to be seen.

These are not in any way to be misjudged or misconstrued as another set of contradiction in terms. Somehow, these would be a set of true alarm and emotions, seemingly contra dance though, but quite contradictory in principle.

In like token, however, issues at hand, the problems receiving the real burning flames of their tests could blaster one's emotions and scatter, in passing, the faith, motivation and even the vibrant belief system of those in these examination halls of life.

Kingsley, as noted, was an invaluable asset to the people of Olarkwudo. The Pirate Duke, Duke Mento Mino knew it. He regarded Kingsley with inner admiration. By his nature, greed ruled his better instinct. Therefore, it was, to him, more preferable to use him as a tool to create great misunderstanding than not to take the needed risk.

According to the plan, his fisher-warriors would pitch for the bait; and Kingsley, as you know, was the bait to be caught; and that by the powers of their patient skills. These fisher warriors, one would sooner than later come to understand, were men who were highly trained terror-makers, endowed with all manners of cunnings, even to the very cores of their individual hearts.

Mishap, as ever, has ever been one of the things that could happen to anyone, irrespective of his natural talents, skills and personal trainings. Duke Mento Mino was not, however, unaware of this either. He knew there were some possibilities for disappointments. However, his disappointments in past wars of conquest made him a lease on courage – A courage enough to organize his thoughts in crises, offload his heart-loads in times of reasonings. Thus, helping him to organize and streamline his struggles, past, present, and those that would confront him. He knew what he was doing; And he knew what he was capable of doing; he knew too his personal and his Kingdom's limitations.

He knew himself to be a sharp operator on the road to face the shrewdest dealers of his time. Kingsley's dealings in uniting his own father, the King with the Kingdom where he was learning claimed a unique credit well known to all. So, he would not leave anything to chance. At least, experience had taught him so.

CHAPTER EIGHT

Kingsley was a man who was truly determined to show promise. On the other hand, Duke Mino knew the only way to stop him was to ruin him. He also knew destroying him without keeping him in his custody would not be of much help in accomplishing the greater part of his objective: To monitor the reactions that Prince Kingsley's sudden disappearance would ignite.

"Take him by surprise" the Duke warned the warriors before they left his Dukedom on the "operation friendly mission". They had done such a dirty job before. And they were ready to do it again.

Consternation was the name of the game.

"I came here to learn, not to reveal" protested Kingsley to his captors.

"You are a captive. You must do as we say. Otherwise, we will behead you" responded one of the four men who bound him.

"What are you doing? I'm not sure you know. When the news of this abduction reaches my father, he will send all of you to the gallows" an angry Kingsley called the bluff.

Hardly had he finished his statement when one of the men slapped him on the face. "Why not call your father now?" the slapper dared him. It suddenly dawned on Kingsley that his ex-friends, those with whom he ate and drank, emerged, through some radical metamorphoses, a set of new men with no bon ton at all. Another captor speedily hit him with an iron rod.

"You are Kingsley. We've heard everything about you. Very intelligent, aren't you? You are not from here, are you? To apple Lion, you're spoilt brat of King Bingo; ain't I r-right about t-t-that?" the captor who was stutterer stuttered.

"How dare you call me a brat?"

"Shout ---rup?" the stammering captor hit him again.

"Please let me go. How much do you want?" Kingsley pleaded with them. Since calling a bluff could not help, he reasoned, perhaps bribing them with some ransom something would appeal to their sense of greed. They ignored him. He was disappointed.

To his total dismay the captors had no interest in wealth. They had a different agenda, a higher allegiance to someone, who might be richer than his own father. Who could this be? Who's the brain behind this? He thought real fast: this thought horrified him.

His captors were equally fast but in their actions. Now Kingsley knew it was all over. He was done in, done for, and a goner too. Now he also dreaded his former friends. He became more than ever aware of the fact; he would only be adding pains to his agony by arguing with those who held him hostage.

New terrifying ideas rushed into his mind and began to torment him. "These men were monsters, why did you be-friend them in the first place?" After all, he knew them for three winters in all.

"There was no reason to trust them at all".. Besides, he was in a foreign land. "Not even your host, King Batuque knows what's up now, if you die, who will find out? Why did you do this thing to yourself? Are you a dummy? You should have known better than that?" These spankings by his inner being were more painful than the beatings he received from his captors. "So, what's the use? I can't help you" the smaller, nasty, inner being said again. "Oh dear, why not let me go! Please forgive me if…" Kingsley began to plead again for their mercy. But his pleading was hopeless.

Kingsley was chained, hand and feet. He was carried shoulder high and dumped inside buggy connected to a couple of sturdy black horses.

His mouth was fully gagged with cotton. And his lips were taped down with a glued black ribbon. Two of the men entered the buggy's compartment, one on each side. Then the two doors were closed.

Then a captor served as a driver; while the fourth, the stout-looking stutterer, changed his apparel, and adorned himself like a merchant.

The driver took his position. The tough-looking captor turned merchant sat on a cozy seat between horse, buggy and his merchandise – the gagged man and two men.

Away the horse and buggy driver whisked the galloping horses on their way.

CHAPTER NINE

A month later, Kingsley was still in the hands of the man, Duke Mino, who was the brain behind his being abducted.

"Aha, welcome my enemy" said the Pirate Duke when the exhausted captive was dragged to his presence.

"Where am I?" Prince Kingsley replied.

"Soon you will know. Boy, you are the man who holds the key to my destiny. If you co-operate, we will spare your life and reward you richly. But mark my words; if you venture to play tricks with me, to God who made me, you will die a painful death" the man whose name he did not know vowed.

"What do you want? What do you want from me?" tired but irritated, Kingsley managed to ask.

"Are you not Kingsley, the demon of two Kingdoms…?"

"Don't call me a dem…"

"Sit your mouth down", one of the Pirate Duke's guards rebuked Prince Kingsley. He supported his command with two lashes of a cane. It stung Kingsley pretty bad.

He was virtually starved on the way to this place, receiving a crummy piece of food, once a day, during the whole journey. It was not just that the food did not taste good; it was not big enough to fill up the stomach of a hungry child, speak-less of a famished man.

Kingsley endured the whole ordeal. In all his life, that was the first time other people had insulted and mistreated him with that degree of impunity.

"What have I done to deserve all these?" Kingsley stretched out his two hands in search of their justice.

"You deserve these because you hold the key to my destiny" the man in purple robe replied.

Kingsley looked confused. And the man who just told him read the expression on his face.

"Boy, soon you will understand. I will give you time to think. You will recall for me all you know. You will provide me every pertinent information about your two Kingdoms, their wealth, their warriors, and their strategic locations…"

"I can't provide that, that's privileged information…"

"Yes, you will. Don't play tricks now, boy" the Pirate Duke disagreed. And one of the Pirate Duke's guards approached Kingsley with a drawn sword. Kingsley was terrified at the sight of the blood-stained blade.

"Please, I will do my best" Prince Kingsley begged for his own life.

"I know you would", the iron-willed Pirate Duke agreed with a terrifying smile.

"I will leave you to do a thorough thinking. You have my mandate to appear here tomorrow, His Highness" the Duke bowed, and his sudden change of attitude made Kingsley to realize his worst fear – Indeed this man must be the famous Pirate, Duke Mino.

As the Duke began to walk away, Kingsley summoned up courage to ask a "pertinent" question.

"Sir, how can I do a clear thinking when I am not free?"

"His Highness, you are about as one the freest Princes I've ever seen. Your brain, mind and imagination can travel to any place in the whole universe without inhibition. Beside you will use your mind to think, not your legs, nor your hands. Bye, Your Highness" the Pirate Duke made his exit.

Kingsley saw that his hope of being unchained was an abortive one. If the leader of this group, this human-demon, would not be considerate enough to set his legs and hands at ease, Who then would? It was a lost hope, and a pathetic case. He would have to obey them, per-adventure, he would be saved at last.

When the Pirate Duke was gone, the guards dragged Prince Kingsley back to his cell. It was a specially designed dungeon, three flights of stairways for three storied, underground, beneath the surface of the soil. It would have been a useless exercise to dare an escape because the dungeon was simply secure. For example, there were ten iron bared compartments that led to the cell where Prince Kingsley was roomed.

At the first gate were stationed ten-armed security men; they were, combat-ready, around the clock. At the second underground gate was even a tighter security. There were twenty hefty men in in variety of warriors' outfits. Each of them held a specially trained attack-dog to its leash.

The third gate provided a different security scenario: Two monster-like she wolves stood guard. Kingsley could not, in his lengthiest imagination, depict how those monsters came to be there. The fourth gate gave an impression of safety. But, beneath this deceptive aura were specially set-iron-traps. Each of which could cut an attempting escapee in two halves.

Coming to the fifth gate, one saw a different security system or measure. There were thousands of blood-sucking rats. These rats were bred and trained through a special genetic engineering.

These specially trained rats could jump at anyone attempting to escape, bite, and dig in their mouths, and sip all his blood, leaving him lifeless before he could even make his way to the sixth gate.

The sixth gate was a pure terror. A total darkness coupled with ghost-like voices did abide here in plentiful proportion. How the people got all these security systems, Kingsley could not fathom.

Seventh gate offered a surprising gate of contrast. An intense light and a scorching heat would easily intimidate anyone who dared to escape from this location.

As one reached the eighth gate, one saw the busts of the Pirate Duke rotating around him. It was a clear signal and a constant reminder of who was in control. There were more than twelve busts. Amazing though, each of these twelve busts could speak in a human voice. And each bust emitted a blinding ray from its eyes. They could easily confuse or kill someone who was attempting to escape.

The ninth gate looked simple but terrible. Ten armed men were here, a replica of the first gate. But the pure mark of contrast was that the security men at this gate were very friendly, cordial and courteous.

At the tenth gate were a couple of the most beautiful women Kingsley had ever seen. They were so beautiful that a saint could readily forget all the horrors and lust his soul after them.

These women were there to keep Kingsley company. They were eager and available whenever he needed them. They were commanded to provide for his sexual needs. They smiled, danced, sang and did anything that would make him cheerful.

The two women were so friendly to distraction. But, in fact the Pirate Duke planted the spy-women to prod his mind, or the mind of any other most-needed prisoner of his time.

All the guards in this under-ground dungeon worked an eight-hour shift before another set of guards would take their roles. In effect, Kingsley was able to see six different most beautiful women, daily, night and day.

At the end of each shift, the two women reported directly to the Duke on everything that happened during their shifts.

It was always a mystery to Kingsley how the every-two pretty women could get through the dungeon's security gates with neither the she-wolves nor the blood-sucking rats doing them bodily harm. It was also a mystery to him how they got him through those intimidating gatekeepers to put him in the cell where he roomed.

As the days passed by, Kingsley became more thoughtful than ever. He was suspicious of the women, though they gave him everything a man would desire in a woman. Though the planted women did their job, daily, with a keen sense of professional touch, he sensed that something was amiss, and he became withdrawn.

Kingsley began to remember the crimes of his father as well as the war crimes of his adoptive father. He wondered whether he was being punished by nemesis because of what they did. This thought alone made him to despise himself for admiring the men who he once regarded as his heroes.

He recalled how his own father offended the Oracle, killed the pythons, murdered the Chief Priests, and insulted the ancient spirits that looked after the universe. Also. he remembered the treacheries of his adoptive dad, the King. His fearful mind drew a graphic picture on how he beheaded his fellow human beings in the battles…And how human heads were presented to the King's then King for selfish glorification. As he recalled all these horrors, he feared for the worst.

CHAPTER TEN

When the war broke out between the two Kingdoms…Bingo's Kingdom and Batuque's, no one was able to figure out Prince Kingsley's where about. It was, however rumored that King Batuque's men who resented Kingsley assassinated him. But even with this unproven rumor, there was no one with tangible evidence to substantiate its plausibility.

Earlier in the dispute, a trickle-down bloodshed began to show its ugly face. Later, it looked like a riot, giving rise to something resembling a civil war that raged simultaneously in two powerful Kingdoms. One must not forget the role Prince Kingsley played in bringing the two Kingdoms closer together. So, one must also keep in mind the fact that due to this closeness of interaction, there were many people of each of the two Kingdoms in the other.

Before the war began, some high-ranking, diplomatic delegates were dispatched to Batuque's Kingdom to resolve the problem once and for all. This very political maneuvering was a last resort at King Bingo's behest. It was a move painfully made to avoid the potentialities of breaking the much-dreaded Pandora box.

When the diplomatic negotiation failed, the guns and bullets gave way to bitter world of bloodshed. For example, millions of children died, older people died. The warriors too died in record number. There was not the victor, but the vanquished at the end of the war.

The two conquered Kingdoms lost a high record of their lives and a high record of their properties.

King Bingo died during the war, but King Batuque managed to survive. It was a war that opened his eyes to the fact that he was tricked into fighting a war. However, by the time he knew what really happened, it was way too late: Too late that his former best friend, King Bingo, died hating him.

Also, too late that the cunning Duke Mino, at last, came out openly and declared himself solely responsible for the missing Prince. He boldly told the war-weary Kingdoms that he alone had a custody of Prince Kingsley. And too late, most of the resources that the people needed, for survival, were wasted in the needless war effort before the brain behind it, the trickster, showed up. He would have paid back the evil man; but for King Batuque, it was too late.

Hardly had Duke Mino made the revealing declaration, when he declared his own war on the Kingdom of Olarkwudo. For example, he sent his armed warriors; and they came in many a swarm of invasion. King Batuque had his last fight in a battle pitch against the marauding warriors of the great Pirate, Duke Mino. He was captured in that very last battle, hanged publicly, all in total disgrace.

Duke Mino's warriors, later in the day, went on a rampage. They ravaged and ransacked the war-torn Kingdom. Everywhere saw their footprints. The women were raped at sword-points. Captured warriors were beheaded for spots.

Children were forcefully separated from their parents. Those who resisted were hanged like their own defeated king. At the end, Duke Mino's warriors declared themselves the winners of the war. A law was passed giving the entire Kingdom as an inheritance of the Pirate Duke. The violent grab of a Kingdom was sugar-coated an eminent domain of the victorious King.

When this event, which later became known as "victory parade", the pirates, the last invaders, did everything they could, not only to humiliate, but to provoke the helpless vanquished to wrath.

On the first day of the celebration, a holy Sage among the conquered people would be brought to the Public Square. A mock coronation of him would be made. Some of his people would be asked, under threats of death, to perform their native rituals for the mock King. They would dance, prostrate, and chant before him. And at the end of the mock coronation, the holy Sage would be executed by hanging. Thus was the supreme humiliation of the native crown. Thus too, the victors displayed their penchant as the victorious. And thereby they reinforced their victorious position as the new leaders of the land.

Of course, the mock coronation went a long way to break the hearts and the spirits of the conquered people. Also, the same ceremony of humiliation planted a huge cloud of fear into the future resolve of the younger natives who, one way or the other, might have thought of re-claiming their lost kingdom, someday.

One must remember, however, the very moment the Imperial Rod was taken away from the natives' King. The gesture was customarily symbolic, in that not only the King of the people, but also the people of the Kingdom saw themselves as nothing but truly conquered people. The Rod was the symbol of the Kingdom's strength. And the warriors of the kingdom were neither supposed to surrender, nor give up their fight provided the King retained the Rod. They were supposed to die protecting it. They vowed to fight even to the last man and to his last blood.

"To fight to the last drop of the blood" was a significant vow; and such was the most important part of a warrior's mental constitution. The Olarkwudo warriors were like the African soldier ants or termites, which would prefer dying in the defense of their Queen.

The "Grand Parade of Victory" was designed to perpetuate the legacy of the natives' humiliation. It was a bi-weekly ceremony on annual rate. The conquistadors were not only despotic, authoritarian, imperious, but also aristocratic in most things that would bring the natives into feeling bad about themselves. There were some grand designs too, to "civilize and pre-empt" some of the natives' ways into the new mainstream.

These apart, dowsing replaced the magical incantations. Divination became a primitive custom when done by the natives. Indeed, any native caught in such a "primitive practice" was sent to the way of his last King.

Virtually anything which the conquistadors could not understand about the natives was branded as uncivilized. But when a potent natives' herb was successfully pre-empted into the new culture, a fanciful name, rooted in the language of the invaders, was given to the medicinal extraction. And the royal patent would quickly be placed on it to keep the natives away from claiming that their own native herb was useful. And eventually, that very herb, wherever it was found in the kingdom, by virtue of the eminent domain, became an exclusive property of not only the Pirate Duke, but also the fellow whose name was written on the patent certificate.

CHAPTER ELEVEN

One of the earliest things the conquistadors did to "educate" the conquered Kingdom was to establish the "Duke's Order of Travelling Teachers". The aim of this "great" innovation was to "civilize" the "inferior tribes" on the "modern ways" of doing things. This, of course, was a reluctant move to assimilate the invaded natives after so many prolonged years of protests for recognition, respect and better treatment.

Everyone in the Kingdom knew that the least regarded people in the "NEW KINGDOM", as the conquered Kingdom became known, were none other than the true natives.

"If life is a beach, then one must bleach his own". This, in essence, was one of the most popular verbal expressions in the land. The New Kingdom recognized itself. Everyone, in principle, was supposed to cater for his own. But when it came to an issue of unity of the entire New Kingdom, then, every rat must run in the Kingdom's trail.

A measure of one's social standing was simply based on what the individual had. Of course, putting the natives down, no matter how, was a way many of the people used in heightening their own sense of superiority.

"That's a primitive native" was a common comment from the mouth of most of the self-superior invaders.

One would not forget here though, the natives felt bad, whenever they heard the ugly comment. The natives, however, were once a proud and prosperous people. With a sad stroke of fate, the once proud and prosperous people became poor, proud less pages in their own land.

When the Duke's Order of Traveling Teachers was established, a special commission was set up, to ensure that all the other Kingdoms knew about it. Some literary gurus, ideologists, men and women gifted in word pictures, were hired to write news-releases. They were commissioned to create news on how generous the Pirate Duke's Administration had always been to the primitive natives.

The news went as far as to leak all the unimaginable ways in which the Traveling Teachers were fostering imaginary progress, peace of paradise, and clouds of prosperity…thus *'massively helping the primitive people'* who, without such heavy rain of assistance, would have perished in darkness. This fantastic news went on to confirm a popular saying in the New Kingdom. "Whenever thy finger is generous to a naught, maketh thou the people of the world to knoweth and praiseth thee".

Of all people under the surface of the sun, no people were praise-loving than the people of the New Kingdom. It was a notable sign, an emblem of imperial patriotism that everyone in the New Kingdom must praise it.

Naturally, of course, should the New Kingdom decide to go to war, it then followed that its cause was right. Therefore, everyone had to support and praise it.

The Pirate Duke, according to the New Kingdom's constitution, or "the imperial edict", was above correction. In other words, "the man who happened to Duke the Kingdom would be a leader who would never be wrong" – No matter what.

It was the Pirate Duke's duty to rule the Kingdom the way that cherished his pleasure. And that, a grand design of the subjects to obey him with no question.

Questioning the Pirate Duke was virtually unheard of. And when so, equal to treason.

It was this venerable outlook on the dynasty that made the subjects to obey the Pirate Duke out of fear. Once a group of innocent school children was massacred. This happened when the school children meekly protested against the excess space, and academic luxury in their over-stuffed local school.

Away from their academic ground was a group of the natives' children, hundreds in number, living in chained forest. These kids were terribly deprived of the good things that the free children took for granted. For example, the kids in the chained forest were not even allowed to stray away closer to the exclusive school's ground of the free ones.

These school children were unhappy. This was so, not because they were over-supplied. Somewhere within their child-like conscience was a vacuum that needed to be filled.

In turn, the Pirate Duke promoted every member of his elite Guard who took part in the patriotic exercise. Having so "honorably performed their loyal duty". The potential troublemakers saw the Pirate Duke's anger in action…, a flaming and vengeful writing on the wall.

Many years later, the Pirate Duke began to yield to the pressures of the internal problems. This, due not just because of the minor sporadic protests at home, but in the main, due to the major pressures abroad. When the Pirate Duke answered the call for a better treatment of the natives, the natives were very reluctant to enjoy his very reluctant answer. The original distrust was always there.

In the beginning, the natives were deceived into fighting their best friends. Never again would they trust the "contacts" of those who deceived them. And owing to that original deception, never again had the natives seen the lights of gladness, nor the lights of their past glories.

Besides, the children were fearful of the Pirate Duke. They had heard the news on how his Warrior Guards killed the children who wanted to accept them.

Moreover, the elders were even more skeptical of the Pirate Duke's overtures. They had a lot of things to talk about him. Mostly ills, in the privacy of their chained forests. Because all were not well.

One must remember the beginning of the remnant natives. The once proud but now vanquished. Their pride would not allow them to stoop so low as to accept a hand-out given by a reluctant hand.

Given all things, the elders hardly trusted nor desired him. For example, one native elder summed up his people's feelings on aggregate of suspicious sentiments, all in revealing remarks and soul-searching questions. "The past is history; the history is a scar on us. Why should we trust him? He would not spare his kind when they disobey his own law. How much more ruthlessness would he show on those he does not even like?" No doubt, the people who feared him most had an equal contempt for him.

"Very true. The ghost of our history does not sleep. It comes to us in our nightly dreams" responded a fellow native, rich in old age.

"We cannot call him evil. Let his deeds be his own judge"

"Yes, his deeds are always there with him as his shadow when the sun in the sky is watching every living soul in this universe".

CHAPTER TWELVE

It was a new trend in the land. The conquistadors came with their own things – Customs, religions and material stuff.

Smiling became a mark of a criminal. A gentleman was a man who would show a poker-face, and who was very stand-offish. A lady was a woman who exuded masculine disposition, walked like a man, and claimed her rightful place in her drive for equality.

There was no such thing as trusting one another anymore. True love could only be found between two lovers making love. Even this love affair would only be found between sexually compatible partners, namely, male and male, male and female, and even female and another female. All these became the rights in the powerful land.

The day Kingsley returned was an epoch-making event in the land. Here was a man taken captive by the unknown gang. His sudden disappearance became a prelude to a seven-year war that raged between the two kingdoms he truly loved.

The war was fought with ruthless passion. It was a bitter war, resembling a civil war in two kingdoms rather than between the two. This was because of the generous matrimonial arrangements made by the Prince who later disappeared from the people.

It was during the old-man's winter that Duke Mino decided to set him free. This, two years after the war.

The legend of Prince Kingsley did not die with the ravages of the war. And many times in the land, young children were told many wonderful stories about a young Prince who disappeared. That it was because of his disappearance that brought about the all-time worst war between the former friendly two kingdoms.

Some of the war survivors, however, resented Kingsley ever leaving home to a foreign land. On the other hand, the people from where he disappeared had a mixed feeling about him. A few of the people in this ruined Kingdom viewed him as an angel of bad luck. There were, however, the majority admirers who still held him as their savior who was out to make the two Kingdoms very great. He was, as the people used to say: "A man whose mind was a station ahead of the journey". But Kingsley was not allowed to complete the journey.

Kingsley's father died during the war due to heart break. In those days the sick King would mourn daily the deaths of his warriors. The thought of his King-on-the-line, whose disappearance was at-liberty-to-be- unraveled, added great sorrows to his heavy heart.

The King was a bitter man. He was so bitter because of his son. That alone was a riddle too tough to handle. He was vexed by the burdens of the chaotic war. Chaotic in that the war and its *bitterness had engulfed the once two friendly Kingdoms with seemingly no end in sight.* The King felt betrayed by another King in whom he once reposed with the greatest level of human confidence.

The King's sorrow was coupled with bitterness; the enmity between the two Kingdoms at war was coupled with an abyss of bloodshed. All these troubles combined and consumed the heart of the devastated King. He died a King of sorrow, bitter even at the very point he gave up the ghost.

King Bingo had no personal misgivings against those who truly put him into troubles. Because he hardly knew anything about the elaborate psychological tricks they played on him. If at all he had known, it would have been a very personal fight against the Pirate Duke. Because the latter was the man who deprived him of his son, his peace of mind, his friendship with King Batuque and the lives of his own people. The tricks were so clouded in secrecy in that no one among his own people was in vantage position to give him the slightest clue about it.

King Batuque managed to survive the seven-year war. The great devastation left him a terribly broken man. Weak and his once great Kingdom was totally ravaged, by the war, he was bedridden in the last six months of the war. He aged so fast within those seven years that at fifty, he looked like someone older than the Biblical Methuselah. Dragged out from his sick bed, he was personally beheaded by the Pirate Duke who plunged him into an unneeded war.

Each Kingdom lost more than one-half of its former total population in the war. That was not all. The aftermaths of the war, such as cholera, kwashiorkor and dysentery claimed more than one out of every three who happened to survive the man-made tragedy. Scars of the war printed themselves for all to read. Depigmentation of the last survivors' skins became one of the lasting legacies of the war.

Hunger became a terrible legacy, too. Food was so scarce that some starving women, out of peak desperation, took part in eating their young ones, just to survive.

Nature itself helped to worsen the troublesome situation. There was no rain in the land for five solid years during the devastating, seven-year war. And when the winter did make its appearance, all the snow that fell quickly turned into a cloud of bitter coldness that quickly disappeared into the thin air. This alone made it impossible for the people to gather the snow and transform it into the scarce water.

The natives of the Kingdom could not help but see that their former helpful Great Spirit had abandoned them. They knew it. They said it. And they believed it. The fact that fate goaded them into this weird premise was evident with a heavy burden of perfect proof.

Once King Batuque cursed his personal god for letting him down. Twice he condemned his ancient supreme deity the Great Spirit for allowing the worst of fortune to befall him. He went ahead and accused all the gods, worshipped by his people, for unhealthy conspiracy. And he was desperate, frustrated and disappointed.

"They are no good; they betrayed us who worshipped them the most" the King lamented. His Chief Advisers, the Wise Sages, and even the Necromancers, did not advise him to withdraw his words – Because they equally believed that what the King believed in was the collective view of all the people in the land..

When Kingsley returned from the foreign land, he found the land taken over and ruled by a man more powerful than his adoptive father. Things were no longer as they used to be. He felt a sense of no vindication when he found his real father's Kingdom being ruled by the very stutterer who slapped him.

Duke Mino rewarded his warlord, the stammerer, by making him the Governor of King Bingo's Kingdom. It was a sound blow to his pride to see all his fortunes taken away from him. Kingsley wept.

The invaders from the north had not only taken his homeland, also, they enslaved his people, mostly the remnants. And they ruled his people with an iron hand. It was a tragedy. His adoptive father; the rightful King of his second Kingdom, was not only beheaded, his lifeless body was hanged publicly… hanged on a cross till all the vultures reduced his body into a mere carcass.. All because he refused to renounce his throne.

Kingsley learnt so many tales of sufferings by his dual people. He saw the scars wherever he went. The people who knew him before his disappearance were happy to see him again, but sad that it all came to that end.

He recalled the good times he had with his father, the King. Then he remembered the pleasurable moments he spent with King Batuque, the slain King of Olarkwudo. These pleasant memories changed into a heavy burden, a yoke on his soul. It was this dramatic change, a change from good times to hard times that touched him so deep, so much that he tempted to commit suicide… only to be saved from the tragic death by some well-meaning and watchful friends.

Kingsley learnt to live a life in two different worlds…a royal life and a worst living condition. Once his father was the King of the land…and he was very proud of him. Then his father died a very painful death and the agony of his father's painful death haunted him. He longed for a total revenge. But he did no longer have the means to that end. Most of his people, mostly the remnants, were put in special enclosures, carefully guarded by warriors who were armed and dangerous. The conquistadors viewed every remaining native as a security risk. And he was terribly treated as such. The weak, elderly ones, plus the young child of his native land were scattered to recluse quarters as servants of their overlords. Most of them were beaten to bananas by those who claimed them as their personal pets, pages, slaves or belongings.

There were no human rights for them because the vanquished bunch were tagged as sub-human beings with no human rights.

Oftentimes, travelers through the land would poke fun at the natives, just for the fun of it. For example, "the silly beasts" was a common thing to call the natives. Of course, a traveler would refer to the natives as such whenever he wanted to curry favor with the new owners of the land.

Whenever this happened, the new landowners who did hear him say that would be pleased and impressed. Oftentimes a new visitor would be naturalized. That, with no interview, if he demonstrated his patriotism enough by poking fun at the primitive natives of the land.

"This is a patriotic alien" the greatly pleased Immigration Officer would say and stamp his seal on the visitor's passport. A winter later, the same visitor would be made a permanent citizen, with all powers and privileges. Gifts would be given to him: A piece of land and a couple of the young natives to serve him – One, a teenage girl to service him.

"Love the land or leave the land" was the motto of the conquistadors. Love it for all it stood. Or leave if you disapproved. There was no in-between.

There was a new intellectual program. Every owner of a native person, especially the owners of the young natives, were regularly taught how to teach their slaves that they be grateful, to those who own them, in all things.

Besides, there emerged an idea by a profound philosopher among the elite brains of the newcomers. The newcomers, however, were the hordes of favor-seekers whose patriotic spirits earned a special spot in the hearts of the conquistadors.

This very fellow, a philosopher by profession in his homeland, was a phlegmatic fellow who had no sense of humor to his credit. But here in the New Kingdom, a home for those rejected in their homelands, his idea was lauded as the purest extract of intellectual pool – namely, that "the primitive natives were savages, lunatics and wild animals on the edge of extinction – That the conquistadors were the sole saviors and the only redeemers of an ape-like race that were promptly delivered from their own hands".

The Pirate Duke was so impressed by this ideological breakthrough that he felt he was right, in the first place, by tricking the two Kingdoms into a seven-year war. He invited the eminent scholar to a royal banquet. The Pirate Duke personally introduced the phlegmatic fellow as "a great philosopher" to his distinguished guests at the banquet. Sooner had this happened, than the humorless fellow became a pinnacle of idea in the New Kingdom.

Another high thinker came up with a new idea – That a disease was about to break out – A disease which would have spelt a disaster for the ape-like race in feather clothes. That the doom was just about to happen, when fate used the conquering Duke to deliver them. This latest idealist went ahead to propound how loving the early conquistadors were – And how the averted deadly disease, which was about to strike, would have been.

While these ideologists were breaking gold mines from the heart of the Pirate Duke, few of the elderly natives who could recall, through distant memories, knew how the last invaders came, were fearful to disagree. For example, they were fearful for their own nearly wasted lives. Even if they dared to speak out, no one would have listened to, or agreed to their version of the events. After all, the conquistadors were in total control. And as the saying went in the land:

"He who holds the sword, holds the pen". With sword he could uphold the law, and with pen, pen down the way he wanted the history to be known.

With the passage of time, the religious bodies made themselves more available to the New Crown. For instance, the years the various institutions were reluctant to get involved had passed away.

It was easy, as they found out, to make it in the New Kingdom. After all, the land became rich, mostly by acquired goods. That, by piracy. Then, the people could make it by jeering the scapegoats, the primitive natives, and by praising the Pirate Royal, the Redeeming Duke.

There was a keen sense of competition between the various institutions, the several interest groups, to be-friend and to please the Royal Duke. And the religious authorities became the tools in the hands of the Royal Duke. He would wield them the way a good sword user would do in a battlefield. And they were happy to be in his service.

The religious powers were subject to the power of the Royal Duke. And just as the dungeon's young women, planted by the Royal Duke to spy on Prince Kingsley during his years in the underground cell… They were all answerable to the Pirate Duke.

To appease the Royal Duke, the theologians came up with a new idea on how to look at things in the New Kingdom:

. "Everything good is of God, everything evil is of the devil, and the devils are of the primitive natives". But, the poor, conquered natives could neither disprove nor protest against that.

Again, the theologies made another breakthrough. For example, 'everything good and strong are of God; everything bad and weak are of the devil, therefore the natives belong to all the devils'. So easy, the new discovery became the popular wave of the Kingdom. New visitors to the land loved and sang the songs of the peak discovery…because it gave them an enormous opportunity to curry favor with the Supreme Ruler of the land.

The natives who had already seen themselves betrayed by their own gods and Great Spirit saw themselves as the theologians saw them.

CHAPTER THIRTEEN

Among the gifts of the conquerors were the new churches, factories and job opportunities. For example, when you worked, you get paid something which they called "money".

This thing, "money", was a remarkable and an invasive measure by which the old trade by barter was rendered useless. The dead method, based on "you give me your goods, I give you mine, if you and I agreed" was not allowed another daylight. And this happened the very moment that the Duke's Bank introduced some paper-like currency notes and metallic coins into the New Kingdom.

One must not forget, though, that the old system was not only so slow, but truly a laughing-stock form of transaction.; that the natives' trade by barter was contemptibly regarded as the zenith of a primitive culture, was definitely an understatement.

Working became a necessity; and if you really wanted to climb the economic ladder of the Kingdom, then, you must not only work to survive but also work to thrive in the Kingdom. By law, the natives were not allowed to work, because the Leaders of the Kingdom did not consider them as pure human beings. But by the King's minor-edict, the natives could be allowed to have the jobs which the descendants of the conquerors would not accept to have.

A great wave of new problems invaded the Kingdom. For example, many sexually starved prostitutes came into the Kingdom. They came from all the other conquered Kingdoms. As a result, the population of women in the Kingdom increased rapidly. Then, there were fewer men, and more unmarried women. A lot of the prostitutes gave birth to many children. As a result, the rapid population of the children became even higher than total population of both men and women. And they grew up. Some of their daughters began to follow in the footsteps of their own mothers. Social vices were plenty, because the struggle for survival became tougher and tougher every day. Some of these women were young and apish; some were middle-aged and needy; and some, genuinely professionals.

A special Commission was set up by the Royal Council to house the harlots for the working men. The men could go in to them, pay them for some period of sexual expression or relaxation – depending on what you want to call it.

A casual conversation between a worker and a harlot could easily lead to a romantic encounter. It would not matter whether they had known each other before or not. However, they would go ahead and do as their natural desires demanded.

Some would do it in the streets, by the roadsides, in the public parks, and even in their places of worship. In times like these, the religious authorities were supposed to cover it up, unless done by the natives. In which case, the native would either be hanged or jailed, if a man. But if the sinner were a common woman, then, the woman would automatically be set free.

CHAPTER FOURTEEN

She was a woman whose heart was loaded with fear, concern and care. She was also a fortune-hunter and proud of it. On the day she met the Royal Pirate Duke, she was not ashamed to propose to him. She was not ashamed to tell him that she desired to marry him because of fame, power and money.

On the other hand, the Pirate Duke extended his kindness by accepting her as one of his royal concubines. He was also crafty and rebuking in the whole process.

"That's a cheap shot, is it not my dear?" said the Royal Duke.

"Your Majesty, every woman, no matter her status in the Royal Kingdom, desires one thing above all things in her heart" answered the ambitious harlot.

"Could you please tell me what it is?" asked the Royal Duke.

"Your Majesty, even though I have made the singular desire of my heart known to you, it is still an uncommon honor to repeat my request before my King. Therefore, Your Royal Majesty, may I become your new bride?" responded the bold harlot.

"My goodness. I have never met a woman who is so determined to become a Queen. I am impressed. I shall give you a chance. For now, you are welcome to be one of my Royal Concubines"

"Thank you so much, Your Majesty. I shall not disappoint you" responded the brave harlot.

"That's alright. And from now onwards, feel free as well as feel at home in my Royal Palace. One of my Royal Guards will show you your Royal Quarters. And at my pleasure, you will be invited to grace my Royal Chambers"

"Thank you again, Your Majesty" responded the harlot.

"My dear, you are welcome" said the Pirate Duke.

"I cannot wait to hear my name be called, on that special day, as the favored concubine to grace His Royal Majesty's Royal Chamber" said the harlot.

"Well, with your wit and wisdom, so far, it would not be a bad idea for your King to make a few exceptions to the Royal Protocols. Now, for you, you are welcome to my chambers at your best of wishes" said the Pirate Duke.

"Thank you so much Your Majesty" said the newly made Royal Concubine. She was so happy. And she was truly elated. She would graciously step in at the Royal Pirate Duke's

annual banquet. She would enjoy the Duke's royal bosom; a number among the Duke's other lovers.

A woman on a mission: Here was a woman who could not hesitate to use her suddenly acquired influence to hurt any man who she suddenly disliked. Mr. Kukumba was unlucky enough to fall into her trap.

"I was very tired yesterday, I needed love. But you were a no show. What's the matter with you?' she said.

"You're right. You're right. But let me say one thing: I want to marry you. But you keep on seeing another man. How do you think that makes me feel?" Governor Kukumba asked his live-in lover.

"Don't be silly. The Duke does not even know you. He…"

"…What are you talking about? You are my future wife. He should respect my feelings".

"My soul is in trouble, oh, my legs hurt" she changed the topic.

"They hurt because you used them with the Duke. I wish you're a faithful would-be wife"

"Don't be silly" she was offended by what he said. "Don't you see what we are doing? Is there any difference? You dumb. Oh, take it easy, I'm not running away".

"Give me the thing. Quit complaining, will you? When you do it with other men, do you complain this much?" the Governor was indeed a jealous lover.

"I'm fed up with you. Let me go. By the way, I repented last Sunday morning during mass. What we're doing is wrong. We are sinners. Don't ya get it?" said the harlot.

"We are only making love" the Governor said

"Yes?"

"The Bible told us to love" said the Governor.

"So?"

"Are we not making love – Loving one another, you my neighbor loving me. Me your neighbor loving you" answered the Governor.

"We are not married. Your reasoning is twisted. We shall go to hell because of this" said the harlot.

"You are kidding. You don't know what you are talking about" said the Governor. Another insult on his part. She did not like it.

"It's you who don't know what you are talking about" she pushed him away and his thing came out of her thing.

"Why are you doing this to me?" the Governor protested

"Because we are doing the wrong thing"

"But you initiated it. You asked me to go to bed with you. Didn't you?" the Governor asked the harlot, resting his case in the process.

"Yes. Because I needed a man at that moment. But now it is a different story. Leave me alone, will you? If you keep on arguing, I will shout "rape" and you will be put in jail for the remainder of your miserable life"

"I'm sorry it has all come to this"

"Will you shut up?" she shouted

"I don't like the way you're ordering me around. I don't like it a bit" the Governor protested.

"You go to hell" the harlot shouted, firmly.

"What?" the Governor retorted

"I said, 'go to hell'"

"Make sure you don't repeat that. It's insult. And I will not take it from you"

"You can't argue with me in my bed, my room and my house. It's all mine. Now off, or I'll call the cop". But "my house" was not true; the house belonged to the Governor.

"Please take it easy. Remember we're lovers" the man's angry voice changed dramatically

"It's all over" she pushed him

"Don't push me" the man protested

"Twag" she slapped him in the face

"Twag, twag, twag" the man returned her slap, three dirty times in a row.

"Yee-e-eh" she burst into crying. She ran around the big rooms in the Governor's house. The Governor gave her a chase. She was much younger than the old Governor. As such, she ran faster than the old man that pursued her. She grabbed a book from the Governor's bookshelf. And before she could throw it at him, the Governor caught her hand and removed the book from her. She ran again, yelled out again louder. Her man, so close to her heel, both naked.

While the fighting was going on, a neighbor who overhead them called the cop. There were two policemen at the door when the Governor opened the door.

"Sirs, may I help you?" the Governor asked them. By this time, he was half-naked.

"Someone called us, Governor. Any problem?" one of the cops asked

"No, just a minor disagreement" he tried to take charge of the whole situation

"I see" the cop replied. The two police officers were about to leave when the woman burst into another yell.

"Is she O.K?" the two policemen asked spontaneously and rushed straight into the house

"He raped me" she lamented to the cops. "Rape" was a major crime in the land. Only the crowned Duke could get away with it.

"Really?" the two officers asked simultaneously

"He nearly killed me. He choked me. He hit me. He kicked me. He slapped me. He squeezed me. He twisted my arms. Oh, my legs hurt. He almost killed me…" she accused him in a row.

"Why did you do that?" one of the two police officers shouted at the Governor.

"I didn't do that. It's all lies" the man shouted back at the Police man.

The police glanced back at her. But the naked woman made a sign. It was that type of sign that a woman, in terrible painful labor, makes at the sight of a mid-wife: yes to a woman who would understand that all she needed was not argument, but a total deliverance.

"My friend, I have no choice but to arrest you until you prove your innocence" the policeman came closer to the surprised Governor. "Turn your back and put your hands to the wall, will you?"

"Look officer, it's all lies. She is my girl. We're engaged to be married…"

"You can tell the judge or your lawyer that. I'm just doing my job"

The Governor was arrested and taken to the police custody. Here was a man who was seen as a god by the natives many years ago. He was a man who would have continued to be the loyalist, the man personally hand-picked by the Duke to be the Governor of Olarkwudo.

Governor Kukumba messed up the whole show. Yes, he did because of his blindness in the life of an unfaithful woman. He forgot there were more than one woman to a man in the vast land. His blindness earned him the rage and anger of his own boss. He went into a woman who was the Pirate Duke's special concubine. He made love to her. He got engaged with her, and only to be ruined by her.

CHAPTER FIFTEEN

Mr. Kukumba was a man reputed for his Midas touch. Once he was captured in a battlefield. Through a natural force of circumstance, namely, a strong wind from the South turned his leading captor into loving and worshipping him.

It did happen in the early stages of the great invasion. For example, Captain Kukumba was one of the warriors from the North who came to conquer the Kingdom of Olarkwudo. He met Kingsley in the dungeon and learnt much about the Kingdom from him, via, the women planted by the cunning, Pirate Duke. And in the early stage of his military career, he became a friend and a trusted Adviser to the Pirate Duke. However, like other advisers, neither he nor his co-Royal Advisors was held in total confidence.

Yes, Captain Kukumba was a leader of a military contingent. His contingent was made up of a few, specially trained fighting men. They were sent out on a fact-finding mission, known as "rekki". Indeed, they were a group of special spies, sent real deep into the enemy territory. In a conventional war, only ten or less people would have been sent on such a vital mission. Here, however, was a different kind of war.

"Kill everything that stands on your way" was the order from above. Clearly this type of war was the type of war in which a warrior was fully prepared to either kill to survive or be killed by the enemy.

"Operation no mercy" was a response the owners of the land gave as their counter offensive. They knew they had lost so much; but they were still proud enough to know that the land was theirs, as such, their responsibility to defend it.

Captain Kukumba was in this type of situation – In a jungle war, which its motto was: kill or get gone.

Despite all the losses in the seven-year war, the natives fought gallantly to defend their own land. For example, their teenage boys and young women willingly volunteered into their Kingdom's groups of trained warriors. They fought their common foes with uncommon valors.

Captain Kukumba and five of his men were captured. When Kukumba and five of his men were captured, by the natives, there was no doubt in their minds that they would be killed. Even prior to the last battle that turned them into mere enemy captives, Captain Kukumba and his men were surrounded. They fought so hard and escaped. Then, they came back with more fighting men to confront the native warriors that once surrounded them. They pitched a fight with a swarm of arrow throwing-enemy warriors. Captain Kukumba and his men had long guns and pistols, the better weapons their enemies could not even manufacture.

During their fiercely fought battle, Kukumba and his men killed not less than a hundred of the enemy warriors. This bravery was done before their enemies succeeded in surrounding them for the second time. And this time, the native warriors did not allow them to escape. Rather, they subdued Captain Kukumba and his last remaining men.

The ratio of the enemies' death to the Kukumba's men felled in that battle was approximately seven to one…which in fairness to a military expedition, underscored the gallantry of the invaders from the North.

Five weeks in captivity, a strong wind from the South wrecked a salvo type of havoc on the tents and dwelling places of the defenders of the vast land. The natural phenomenon caught everyone by surprise. So off-guard was the invading natural salvo in that so many people were killed.

To the captured prisoners of war, Kukumba and his men, such a natural event was called a devastating "tornado". On the other hand, the natives viewed it as nothing less than the 'wrath of the Great Spirit'. To them, nothing should be done about it, safe to let the Supreme Deity exercise its wrath without human intervention.

In those days, however, legend had it that it's only an untouchable messenger of the Great Spirit that could intervene in such a circumstance. That this messenger was nonetheless, "Equal to the Great Spirit", but so chose to serve him.

For some time, then, the natives had not seen any of these spiritual messengers come down to help them. But somehow, they continued to believe in their ancestral message, the oral heritage passed down from generation to generation.

When the hurricane and its tornado were doing their job of devastating the land, Captain. Kukumba emerged to the rescue. He removed the fallen tents from the bodies of the natives. He removed the sands which were in the eyes of the hurricane victims. This he did by blowing a mouthful of air into their eyes.

In the past, such victims would have been allowed to go blind. And no one would have helped because they were under the wrath of the Great Spirit.

But Captain Kukumba did the unthinkable. For example, he ran to the weeping children of his captors, the natives and consoled them. To the natives, his kindness was nothing but an act of the legendary messenger. And as such, they viewed his kindness as a great conflict between the angry Great Spirit and a messenger of the Great One.

When the damaging wind was through with its job, Captain Kukumba's captors summoned him and his men. Their natives and their children were also gathered in a special place. They were all gathered to honor and adore Captain Kukumba and four of his fellow prisoners.

And as Lead Warrior Kukumba and fellow captives watched a sudden change in their captors' attitude…they were equally unable to communicate in their different language. However, they noted that something was radically amiss, different and totally unusual.

"Arigatho Chi chi. Chokom batubo u y lai ka himo" the lead captor said. After the un-interpreted statement, the native people prostrated before the war captives.

Again, the lead captor said the same thing in slightly variant tone. The people, men, women and children rose to their feet. Again, they knelt down; then, they prostrated before the captives once again. They did this for seven times before they stopped their ceremonial worship.

After their profound obeisance, a golden chair was brought to the village square.

"That chair is made of pure gold" one of the captives pointed out to Captain Kukumba to see.

"Wait, let's see what they're going to do with it" Captain Kukumba replied to his fellow captive.

"I wish I could lay my hands on it" said the captive.

"It's worth a King's ransom" Captain Kukumba estimated the "worth" of the golden chair.

Again, the lead warrior said something which the captives did not understand. All that Captain Kukumba and his fellow captives could figure out, when the man said something, was that he looked cheerful. At the end of the lead warrior's short speech, which happened to be a set of instructions, his men reverently carried Captain Kukumba in their hands and placed him on the golden chair.

Again, the lead warrior issued another chain of commands to his people. Soon after his commands, four other golden chairs were brought in. These four chairs looked less dignifying than the one on which Captain Kukumba was made to sit on.

Two of the chairs were placed beside each side of the man on the executive golden chair. In other words, two chairs on each side. Again, the lead warrior's men carried the four captives reverently and placed each of them sacredly on their respective chairs.

Having placed their divine messengers on their due seats, the natives renewed their united Spirit of worship. They added more and more pomp and varieties to their spiritual merriments: Dancing and spreading their pincho garments before their gods and clothing these gods with their newest pincho garments were part and parcel of their ceremonial worship.

To the outside world – a world far beyond the realm of this ancient Kingdom, the invaders from the North were a herd of merciless criminals. But here they were, five in number, being worshipped as true gods.

It would have been unheard of for a member of these "criminals" to ever conceive of civilizing the very people they intended to invade, in any way.

Ironically, life became something of a mystery when Captain Kukumba became a captive in the land of invasion. He could remember how badly some of those who were now worshipping him slapped him and his men when they were captured. It seemed strange to him, how a natural salvo, namely tornado and a strong wind, could not only change the trend of things, but also influence the natives' perception about the very enemy warriors who came to kill them.

Initially, there was an air of confusion. Followed by a pleasant surprise. Then a total sense of joy. Most of all, the third, in being worshipped, by one's enemies, as their gods.

Captain Kukumba did not waste any time in taking a total advantage of the changed situation. He assumed, to aggregate proportion, in his supreme endeavor to exploit the new situation to the fullest.

As he learnt beforehand, "a man whose fate has presented with sweet grapes must be crazy to seek for the sour ones". Captain Kukumba knew this to be true in every way. After all, at least, he had known the new, sweet gift of his personal fate. After all, he had become the merciful god of his own true enemies.

When Captain Kukumba stood up from the golden chair, the natives bowed and prostrated. They did so, all in total reverence. When he raised his two hands heaven-wards, the people reverently stood, their heads bowed towards him, and they did as he did.

He walked regally to an armed warrior. He drew the warrior's sword from its sheath. Then he walked away with the sword back to his throne. And he put the warrior's sword right in front of his exalted chair. Then he sat again.

Sooner had he done so when the entire worshippers took off their swords and brought them to the foot of the throne. Captain Kukumba sat and watched. He sat and watched the foolish natives surrender their most powerful weapons to him, who did not like them in the first place.

While he watched, he gauged their response, latent suspicion of his ploy, but the people were all completely taken in by his charm. He told his men, four of them, to begin to improvise a song. They did. And it turned out to be a fabulous idea. They sang. They clapped their hands too. The natives who knew nothing of what they were singing joined in the merriment.

The captives began to dance as they sang and clapped their hands. The natives followed suit, humming the songs, clapping their hands and dancing to the music in their own way. Some of the natives ran back to the remaining tents and brought their assorted implements of music. Among their instruments were drums, flutes and tambourines. They made more music. The tempo was high; their collective spirit, high too. They danced till sunset; deep into the night, and they extended it all night long.

It was this very exploit, a cunning victory which paralleled, equaled, perhaps surpassed the capture of Prince Kingsley Bingo. This special tact, the use of the common-sense in winning the adoration of one's enemies, as demonstrated by Captain Kukumba, this true victory with no bloodshed, that made him a star in the sight of the Royal Pirate Duke.

Having promised to reward him, Duke Mino made him a true Governor of the people who had already accepted him as a messenger of their ancient god. By the Duke's edict, Captain

Kukumba became the Governor of the Kingdom that Prince Kingsley once wanted to defend with his own life.

CHAPTER FIFTEEN (B)

He was among the very few remnants of the tribes who decided, against all odds, to fight the invaders from the North. Here was a cause, as remote as chances of its success were, turned the few faithful ones into a group of burning rage. Here too were the people who were turning a deaf ear to a wiser caution that their conquering overlords could annihilate them with ease at a slightest touch of provocation.

The people were in a meeting, twenty men in all, working out a plot on how to overthrow a forty-million strong armed people. It was a fact of life, that of all the newcomers to the land, the invaders held the original owners of the land in utmost disdain. For example, killing a native by either the new-comers or by the invaders from the North was not, in all legal matters of conscience, considered a common crime.

A native person in the land was truly considered to be an animal lower in natural wisdom than a common beast. And as such, he was not entitled to his natural place. He was not allowed to leave the beast-like chained forest reserved for him, and his kit and his kin. To see a native in a city was an offence enough that could easily lead to him being lynched.

Despite these limitations, the twenty men were determined to try, at least to give their cause a voice. They had endured beatings, floggings and watching their loved ones being killed with impunity before their own eyes.

They had been given some disease-infected clothes to wear, during the bitter winter. This benevolent grace alone was the weapon that killed their people, in thousands, daily, when some poisoned food did not do sound enough job. When the invaders came, as the latter plot was unraveled, they returned as agents of apologies. They pleaded with the natives that the poisoned food *"was a gross error"*. And to make up for such a gross-mistake, *"the imperial government, out of desire for reconciliation, desire to be forgiven, and in spirit of friendship, generously manufactured, the clothes of variable sizes, as would fit all peoples of the nativity"*.

The natives were deceived, yet again, not knowing what the pretty clothes held in store for them. Besides, it was the cold season, and the natives, naive as they were, accepted the chicken-pox virus infested gifts in good faith. This happened a year before Kingsley's return.

"Leave him alone. He's a regular guy; He understands our point of view". The woman who was sitting next to the angry man in "non-natives allowed" bar rebuked. She had seen Kingsley often in the bar. Although Kingsley saw himself as a native, the operators of this exclusive bar dared not throw him out…just like they had done to the other natives for being in a place they were not wanted.

In the case of Kingsley, it was a different matter altogether. He was, to them, like a tsetse fly perching on the scrotum of a naked man, which, if allowed, would have its way. But if threatened, could result to a greater injury.

"Friend" Kingsley addressed the young woman, giving no heed to the man's insult, "If people regard me as an absolute stranger, do you think I'll turn around and regard them as my guardian angel?"

"I don't think so" the woman answered.

"That was no reason for rudeness" the angry man sitting by her jived in, enraged at being ignored

"Cut it off jerk" the woman charged, showing, in passing, what rudeness was all about.

"You give him a dose of kisses" Kingsley teased, perhaps either to insult him or to humor her, or both. There was something brewing in the mind of the man next to her before they met.

Being the type of fellow, a "subject" that psychiatrists would refer to as "a maniac depressant", it was obvious, and psychologically determinable, that the "jerk" had had repressed unpleasant memories.

The "jerk" barked at Kingsley "come here" as if he were a military drilling Master-Sergeant to his new-recruit in the army. As the addressed heard the "jerk" bark the command, he returned his insult with an ironic touch of humor.

"Feliz Navidad"

"What fucking language is that, stupid?" the insolent jerk asked Kinsley

"Shut up dog" the woman addressed him.

Having heard her call him "dog", the "jerk" began to behave like a rebuked dog which desired to please its master. His angry face thawed. His mood in effect changed. He smiled for the first time to Kingsley.

"There you are" Kingsley pointed a finger at him, then made a "V" sign for victory with a couple of his fingers.

"Some people were talking about kisses over there" the smiling dog radiated.

"Right" she agreed to.

"There you are" Kingsley said to her.

She understood that Kingsley was placing compliments on her for her taming the jerk-like dog.

"But this one is different" the woman said. She said so to change Kingsley's an already formed impression of the jerk.

"Different? How? You started it, didn't you?" Kingsley used the word "you" to refer to "him". He did so to confuse the "jerk" from knowing they were talking about him. But the dog was smarter than that.

"I guess I'm wrong. Why don't we make a truce?" the tamed dog said. Kingsley was caught. Still, he wanted to control the damage.

"We are not fighting. Any". Then he turned his face from the changed jerk to the woman. "I am only interested in you as a man would in a woman that captured his fancy"

"I didn't know you liked me so much, Kingsley"

"Not liked, point of correction. You are loved"

The jerk felt threatened by the polished native. He wanted to compete with the new guy...at least, to show he was also a man, for her affection.

"I noticed, my dear, your looks better today than yesterday" the jerk said to her

"That's a double-handed compliment, do you know that?" she rebuked the jerk. And she did not want to give him any room to go further.

"I didn't mean…"

"Thank you though" she sealed him off.

CHAPTER SIXTEEN

"Your lover knows neither Adam nor Eve. All I know is baptize me". There was a roaring applause by the people by the riverside, after the "exceptional native lady" who was converted to Christianity, made this confession of faith.

Since the conquerors' religion came in to the land, this old lady, Mrs. Marina Otirikoyo, could not sleep without being fond of it. She would do anything to defend the interest of the new religion. It was she who exposed the twenty young men, who were plotting to overthrow the government, to the authorities.

She did what she felt that she had to do, because she had learnt from the 'holy book' of the conquerors that a faithful convert must always obey the holy laws. And among the most sacred laws was: "thou shalt not kill". She learnt this at the church. Somehow, she counted it as some heavenly gain when her own people perished at the hands of the authorities because her action promoted peace in the land.

When she turned in the plotters, an escort of armed policemen and a Priest paid her a visit at her residence, to congratulate her. The Priest gave her a book, "How to be a Christian" written by him.

She had been going to his church for fourteen years with no recognition. This time, the man of God was so impressed, he, on the same day, elevated her position in the ministry. Her name was registered in a class of those who would become baptized members of the church. And when baptized, would see herself as an equal to those who ruled the land.

"May the Lord's grace shine upon you. May the Lord redeem you as I baptize you in the name of the Father, of the Son, and of the Holy Ghost". The Priest reiterated when it came to her turn to be baptized. Having confessed Christ as her personal savior before men, she was happy for the moment of her acceptance.

By this time, her body was indeed half-way in the water. The people, the true witnesses to her baptism were standing, watching while heavenly angels rejoiced because her soul was about to be saved from eternal destruction – because the Priest said so.

Having made her confession of faith; the Priest, having presented her, a living testimony before God on high; and the children of God below as the witnesses; the witnesses, after witnessing all that happened, opened their mouths in agreement with the holy Priest; and as members of church, they responded:

"Amen". The woman, Mrs. Marina Otirikoyo did not want to miss the opportunity in saying her own 'Amen' or "may it be so".

She was eager to say "Amen" when the baptizing Priest submerged her remaining body into the water. She could not take it. Something had gone bad while she was completely submerged into the water. She surfaced with a violent splash of water.

Then, there followed the litany of coughing. Some drops of water in the salty river quickly entered into the poor, old woman's windpipe, while she was opening her mouth to join the witnesses in saying her own 'amen'.

And as such, her own "amen" became a vector of uncontrollable coughing. She coughed, so violently in that she became violently uncontrollable. For example, she coughed right in the face of the holy Priest.

"Help me, help" she pleaded as she coughed.

"Oh men, what is this? This is why I hate baptizing these primitive people" the man who authored her copy of "How to become a Christian" allowed his prejudice to take control of his Priestly good manners and patience.

The descendants of the conquerors were kids who found it worthy to reject some of the old values of their forebears. As a result of their deviance, they were called the "new breeds". So many of them truly rejected the hypocritical ways of the Religious

Lords of the New Society. And some of them adopted a new set of behaviors that mocked the esteemed morals of the hypocritical Society.

The New Kids of the Nation were truly different. And some of the things they did, on daily basis, were unheard of when the New Kingdom was a "Class Society".

"These days," as one elderly woman said, "things are no longer the way they used to be. The natives do no longer bow to us when they meet us. They simply walk on the same streets with us. They board the carriage-cars with us. Now, more than ever, they use virtually every amenity we used to enjoy alone. It is a shame our class has changed".

"Why not, ma'am? You came all the way from the Northern Kingdom and stole our land and our blessings. You enjoyed everything that the Supreme Spirit meant, not really for you, but for us. We never chased you away from our land. Now that we are sharing our natural inheritance with the same rogues that impudently stole from us, the same shameless rogues have the guts to complain that life is no longer fair. What a dubious irony. Is it not?" responded a smart native to the self-centered woman.

"I hope you are not trying to insult me. Are you?" asked the woman.

"No. I simply stated the living truth" answered the native man.

"But the way you said it made me look like a common thief. We came to this land with great civilization, true religion, true culture and enlightenment. We developed this New Kingdom; therefore, we should not be seen as a tribe of common land-thieves, or impudent criminals. Should we?" responded the woman with a question. As she spoke, her rage and unspoken words were evident all over on her broad, angry face. Her words were nothing but a rueful commentary, a mournful remark made by someone whose pride and arrogance were violently taken away from her by a lost glory.

Yes, a few winters ago, it would have been an eyesore to see a conqueror stoop so low as to kiss a native girl in public – Safe, of course, to use her as a "pleasure girl" – This he would have done only in the very privacy of his castle – That after flogging a herd of his lazy slaves to motivate them to do their master's job.

"These days, the young men have delved into marriage with the "feather-wearing, dirty natives" at the very expense of their own girls. Worse still, "the ugly natives have become bold enough as to date, kiss and even marry the daughters of their ex-masters. God, we have lost everything". The old woman lamented.

She was angry, very angry at the speedy turn of events, "who could have imagined this happening ten or twenty years ago? It is all because of that radical immigrant, Botamu Jungo, who pushed the Ruling Party over the brink". There was no doubt she hated him. Those who knew Botamu Jungo very well called him "the heavenly warrior" because he took no nonsense from anybody. They said he came as a merchant to the New Kingdom, just to trade.

When he saw what was happening, he decided to change it. He sold his merchandise and used his revenue to fight the system all the way through. Stories had it that his writings irritated the elites of the status-quo.

Being a noble man where he came from, killing him by any means would have plunged the New Kingdom into a no-win war. Therefore, the Great Duke, having studied the whole situation, listened, rather out of fear, to what Botamu Jungo stood for and wanted the Royal Pirate Duke to do.

Micolo Ibukum was a hero of the people in his own right. A proud and a noble man, but a member of the conquered race. Oftentimes he remembered; and he laughed really loud; also, he joked about the good old days. Beneath his jovial face was a dual man full of sorrow and comic strip or comic spirit.

"Life is always a di-synthesis" he remarked quite often. Perhaps he himself knew better what he meant by "di-synthesis".

Among his most popular jokes were the ones he cracked in a town-meeting. This was when his clansmen met in a town-hall to discuss the fate of their remnants in the face of the invaders' new inventions. First, they were mystified by a sight of the man-carrying animal known as "horse" brought in by the invaders. Soon, they learnt how to ride horses.

This time around, the invaders came up with house-like contraction that could do even a better job than many horses put together. To the original natives, this was nothing short of marvel – A marvel testifying to the fact that the conquistadors were superior in every way.

The conquerors were once some killing machines in the guise of mere mortals. Chances were very slim that they would show any act of mercy on any warrior who was fighting on their enemies' side. Today, they've rechanneled their energies to something different. This re-channeling of their wrathful energies was not without some major prices. Prince Kingsley Bingo's legend was there.

The wealthy merchant, Botamu Jungo had enough wealth to buy a crown. But he spent a huge part of his wealth for the cause he believed in. Once, he vowed to buy the New Kingdom into a war if all the amenities were not opened to the natives. The Duke obeyed, because the merchant could have done it.

These days, the natives could have enough reasons to be thankful. They could enjoy a little peace, swallow their bitterness with less harassment; and those among them, who would like to enjoy some jokes, people like Micolo Ibukun, could sit down, spend some time and enjoy their jokes.

"Chase Ipswitch Sharowah" began Micolo Ibukun

"Again" replied the members of the group. By this time, it was time for jokes – Time to laugh at life's vicissitudes.

"In Ipswitch's maternal home, a man who saw a pleasure car for the first time exclaimed 'look, if that thing can run that fast, when it grows up, it will run with a speed so fast that nothing in the whole wide world will be able to catch it". Having cracked this joke on Ipswitch, all the people in the gathering place felled to, and laughed.

When they laughed to their hearts' contentment, Ipswitch Sharowah came up with his own joke – Ready to crack it on Micolo Ibukun

"Chase Micolo" he began

"Again" they answered

"Chase him once more for me"

"A—again" they chorused.

"When Micolo Ibukun was a child, he and his mother visited his mother's lover…"

"Shut up Ipswitch. Don't crack an expensive joke here." The oldest man in the hall stopped him from finishing his joke.

"Yes". The others agreed. Ipswitch was going the wrong path. He deserved the rebuke. And should not contend against it. Ipswitch knew his pride and the respect the young had for the elders. He bowed his head towards the elder who rebuked him.

"Please permit me to start with another one". he pleaded.

"Tell the one that will not be offensive. We have already incurred more troubles in our plates than we can eat". The elder in the midst cautioned. In truth, his remark was an ironic understatement. They did not ask their troubles to come to them. But their problems were unwanted and uninvited guests.

"Please trust me. I will". The young man opened his mouth and closed. Opened and closed again. He looked up, tears filled up his two eyes. The elderly man became aware that his words touched him deeply.

"Sometimes when we don't know what other people are going through, we tend to blame them". The elder began, mindful as he calculated his words.

"Yes, that is true" all the people in the hall agreed.

"We blame a lot" Ipswitch said. Tears still flowing from his one eye. He lost one during the war.

"Someone who had never put himself, his feet in another's moccasins does not know what it means to be in a trying situation".

"You are indeed a wise Sage".

"Yes. Indeed, I am. And we all are".

"The Great Spirit will deliver us".

"Yes, the Spirits of our forefathers are with us".

"It is terrible, though. To be honest as a dove, never in any of our oral history had such a woe befallen our Kingdom. You see, Olarkwudo is no more. Our Great Kingdom is now a history".

"We are under a curse; that could be why. I don't know. But I suspect the Great Spirit has a grudge against us".

"Frustration breeds inertia. Does it not?" asked the Sage.

"Yes, a true saying" another man, a Sage of the conquered people, added.

"Frustration is the mother of inertia".

"You just said it".

"I know. And I wanted you to see what I was saying in a different light".

"We understand" all the people chorused. But the melody of their "we understand" had a mournful tone.

"Our people are demobilized, demoralized and deactivated by the powers of the conquerors; yes, I know. Still, we can challenge them and regain our land" said the brave and bold one-eyed Ipswitch; he was suddenly re-awakened by his ever-brave warrior's resolve. And before the war, he had two living eyes. But after the war, only one was left for him to use.

"Have you seen a toad challenge on elephant? When a toad fights an elephant, know for sure that his lucks of victory are reduced to many zeroes and even to minus zeroes" said a wise Sage. When the Sage finished saying that, all the people bowed their heads in sorrow and heaved their united mournful sigh.

"It's unfortunate" the mournful joker, Micolo Ibukun, intoned. And sad as the rest of the people, he heaved another mournful sigh. All his former beams of smile disappeared from his face. In its place was a stone-faced sorrow.

He looked around. His eyes caught the tears flowing from the eyes of Ipswitch. The sight touched him deeply. His friend's sorrow over-powered his. They were co-warriors in the war.

Mournfully, with tears flowing from his eyes too, he added, "Our pride is gone. The Kingdom Changed".

CHAPTER SEVENTEEN

As the days rolled by, the baptized lady, Mrs. Marina Otirikoyo, became hesitant to go to the church. She was offended, angry and resentful of the whole thing.

She had already begun to question her own rationale in not questioning the truthfulness of the imposing religion. Early on, she would have thought about asking a few heart-turning questions. But the expert, the same Priest who taught his followers, "Blessed are those who believe without seeing" …made her a believer who did not question anything about her new religion. It was because of this smart Christian principle that sunk her desire to see it with her own cultural mirror.

These days around, she truly had enough. She was fed up when those who preached one thing and did just its opposite.

"You want to meet the devil? Then go to the church" she said to someone who came by to tell her she was missed at the church.

To be honest, the native conqueror wanted to know why she had been absent for three consecutive weeks.

"Didn't they tell us not to kill? But they've been killing our people since they came" she asked. She was a native. The conquistador, though a church-going Christian, knew the natives very well. Of course, these natives had a way with questionings and remarks when they wanted to make their points pretty clear. The man did not stay to argue because he knew she was not happy.

When the man was gone, Mrs. Marina Otirikoyo sat down in her hut. She was a childless widow, late in her years. She was aware that many of her own people despised her because of what she had done.

There were those who talked behind her, all in derogatory ways. For example, "She did it because she had no kids". Perhaps she would have killed herself if she had heard such a reflection of herself. "That ruthless witch". Some of them called her at the back. They would have killed her had it not been for their fear of her friends, the makers of laws and authorities. But she got the message in clues and signals.

Kids who used to bow to her, according to the natives' custom, would simply pass by, whenever they met her, without even greeting her. As they said in the land, "Whenever an elder turned himself into a mouse, the children would only have to turn themselves into cats and pursue it". Marina really turned her station to a level less than that of an ordinary mouse. Therefore, the children, who passed her by, were simply fulfilling a role she assigned them to play.

Many of her native friends kept her at arm's length. And almost every native who knew what she did played his part in subtle ways to show his displeasure in her.

On the other hand, most of her friends at the church were not even very friendly. They smiled at her when she was before them, but behind her, she was just another primitive native.

She began to wonder whether she had made a fatal mistake by reporting the twenty natives who wanted to do away with the imperial regime. She searched her heart thoroughly. And she doubted whether the Great Spirit and the church will ever forgive her. She was greatly disillusioned and disappointed in the whole thing. "Why did I do that?" she said to herself. Greed of course. Greed for acceptance. Greed to become like one of those who ruled her. Greed.

From that moment, she saw herself in a different light. She saw the light, and the light was different from the practical light in the church. She saw her true self the way her own people saw her.

She began to blame herself, to cry and to throw her aged body around. Adam and Eve, who she claimed not to know for the sake of baptism, became to her nothing but a part of the whole scheme of deception.

She had seen her native teenage boys tied to the stake and shot to death, just because they smiled at the young women of the conquerors. The boys were accused of sexual misconduct. Then, she had also seen some of the explicit ways the young women and the men of the invaders, even in public arena…without the law of the land frowning at them.. She had seen them misbehave virtually everywhere, including in their churches. She saw no justification in all their moral contradictions.

If they could misbehave in the house of their God, and nothing would be done about it, then, there was no reason to kill some playful children who were just being a bit too friendly…she reasoned in the deepest privacy of her own mind.

There was no limit to the scope of bitterness in the New Kingdom.

"You smile, you commit a crime" said a liberal fellow to an open-minded lady. A middle-aged woman who was fed up with the system, the status-quo. Her daughter was married to a native. And she was happy for them. But her people disapproved and condemned the marriage.

She did not mind what they thought or how they felt about it. She went ahead and gave the happy couple her whole-hearted blessing.

"Are you happy about what your daughter did to your image?" her sister asked her.

"No matter how thin you slice a bacon, they're still baloney" No doubt she was displeased with her question.

"What did you say?"

"I could not believe you could ask such a silly question", she told her earlier. But her sister was a pure racist. "It hurts when people like you support an evil system. Shame on you, when are you going to learn to get along? What is the matter with you?" The bride's mother Monica Von Ihorius was ready for that. It was unfortunate that the first person to voice out against her daughter's marriage was her own sister.

Monica Von Ihorius and her sister had some royal blood. They were daughters of some distant baron and baroness. The two women left their home when they were young girls, fresh out of high academia, in search of new adventure to the New Kingdom.

The older one Monica, was a freelance spirit, while her younger sister, Riki, was more traditional. Somehow, they refused to give up their family name. They retained the title "Von", to show their heritage. Both of them were married. Their respective husbands, descendants of the conquerors. But the men who married them were happy with their wives' titles – "Vons".

"A conspiracy of hope is an embodiment of latent expectation – A vision of the saviors of the oppressed, to redeem the oppressed, and a threat to the oppressors of humanity", wrote the merchant Botamu Jungo. He was hated and loved, feared and admired, rejected and accepted. Maybe he was the compendium of dual-synthesis, or di-synthesis, as the native joker saw it. He made enemies and made friends all at the same time.

"We are the chosen people" she remarked.

"Is that so?" he asked her.

"Yes, that is why we suffer" she said.

"That is quite strange; yes, it is quite illuminating" agreed Kingsley.

"Well, your people say 'he who does not know how to be generous should learn how to return generosities he received from others', am I clear?"

Kingsley found her remark very offensive. Indeed, a red-hot thing in the mouth should not be allowed to stay for long, otherwise, it will not only ruin the taste-buds, it will damage the tongue as well. So, he decided to confront her, right away. Her voice and choice of words were 'clear'.

"Have I ever shown lack of appreciation for any of your kind gestures?" Kingsley asked her.

"No" she answered.

"Then, what do you mean, Flora? That was an offensive remark. I don't appreciate it".

"Please Kingsley. Judge me on my merit. I was not talking about you. You remember that jerk I rebuked at the bar?"

"Oh yes, I do".

"His father is a bishop, a special adviser to the Duke".

"You don't mean it".

"Yes I do. When are you going to learn to believe me Kingsley?"

"It is a pity. I think his daddy did a lousy job on him" responded Prince Kingsley.

"There you go. His father talks about family value and all that stuff. I wouldn't like to marry him. 'He who…"

"Your proverb makes sense".

"Now you understand. Do you not?" said the young woman.

"Oh yes, my love. I sure do".

CHAPTER SEVENTEEN (B)

There was a wave sweeping through the lovely Kingdom. The venerable Royal Duke was alerted, and the masses were not the least uninformed about the new development. People in the high religious altars were sweeping the waves, preaching a cleansing message of moral values.

Here in the Kingdom, a man's worth was determined by what the 'religious moralists' called "'man's moral machorism". Through this new tag, the vain-glorious ladder of masculine elevation became the terror of those in the minority. For example, the male-pimps were scared to death. They had no alternative but to medically, and surgically convert their outer sexual organs into the female type – thereby they became the lesbian identifiers.

The high altars of moral values and their Priests did not hesitate to condemn such a conversion.

Schools in the land were embracing the new gifts of the wave; notably, that there would, henceforth be three forms of families in the land, namely, male-female family, male-male family, and female-female family system. That the new systems should be inclusive and acceptable without any tolerance of discrimination.

Several potentates of the Kingdom clandestinely gave their stamps of approval to the sweeping wave.

"This is our Kingdom. We should be free". One of the potentates declared in a rally. The masses agreed with what he said, almost in unison. There were, of course, a few dissenting voices who saw themselves as the fabrics of morality.

"Freedom without moral limitations is the recipe for social chaos and disaster. We cannot allow freedom where untamed beasts are free to invade every home" said one of the Eminent Moralists of the New Kingdom.

"That is the way it is. Some merchants who cannot tell us the origin of their wealth are pushing our Royal Duke to plunge our peaceful Kingdom into their ocean of madness" responded his fellow Moralist who also came to examine every word the people would say at the public rally.

"Our youths do no longer attend our religious services as they should. During our youthful days, we never said a word back to our parents, especially, on Sunday morning, when our mothers came to our bedrooms to wake us up for morning service. These days, however, our youths would prefer to watch sports rather than go to church to worship God. Ask them why, they would argue that churches in the land are filled with hypocrites"

"Yeah. I sent my first son to a School of Theology. A year into the program, he dropped out, flew over to Jamaica and joined a band of Raggae-demons"

"Oh no. Those people who think that the man of Ethiopia is the real Messiah sent by Yahweh"

"That's right. My son now believes in that nonsense. He called me his 'Jah-man' when I last spoke with him on the telephone"

"Do you think he would repent?'

"I doubt that. He told me that we have broken every moral law in the Holy Book of the Supreme One. When I asked him to give me an example, he challenged me to ask our Imperial Duke to return all the lands we took away from the poor natives. He said that if our Royal Duke and every new alien would not, in collective agreement, return all the lands to what he called the 'true owners of the lands', then, according to him, none of the Pastors, Bishops, and even me, his father, has a moral right to ask him to attend our 'Church of Hypocrites'. That was what he said".

"This is serious"

"Yes, it is. I have poured my heart in prayers, pleading with God to show me how and why we've failed our young ones".

CHAPTER EIGHTEEN

He was wondering what to do with his life when he met her. She was, as the saying went in the land, "a new alibi for a jilted love".

She was indeed a perfect escape for a man who was losing all hope of securing a new "love" once again, in his aging life. The woman was older than he. She wanted a younger man, someone who would give her a new blood.

The younger man was, romantically speaking, in a very bad shape. He was desperate for any love. Age, to him, was irrelevant.

"How are you, ma'am? Please good morning". He greeted her, misplacing the greeting; rather questioning her before greeting her.

"Oh, searching for love, true love" she answered.

"You are at the right place and at the right time" he intimated. Eager to either lead her or to follow her. He was ripe and ready for her love.

"Oh no", she disagreed. "You are working. Beside" she went on to add, rather argue about the weather "it's too hot for love". She and he and a few other people who were standing nearby laughed to their individual heart's contentment. She stalked him away verbally, awaiting him to show her his own stuff. Perhaps she underestimated him. Or maybe, that was her way of preparing her kill, in this case, a young-looking stud.

However, the man had a way with words whenever things involved women.

"Well" he began to say.

"Uh-huuh" she responded.

"We operate on love without season" said the younger man. Then, he turned the people to add a kicker, "Do you all also get a kick out of that?". The young man quite excited at his potential love conquest 'kicked' that back at her. They all laughed, even longer and louder this time. They were gaining acquaintance beautifully. Her words were exciting. So were his. Their verbal exchange excited them in a different plane. They looked at each other's face, then straight in each other's eyes. They felt like they had known each other, being each other's love, for a long time. The spirit of romance was there, playing its blessed games in their individual minds.

Then, his sexual and emotional electrons gained a higher energy level. So did hers. He was a city bobo, and she, a foxy super freak. An expert too. She knew how to control her own thing and wouldn't do it while others were there, watching.

"I shall see you later" she intimated her desire to leave. And as if to show him that she would be his, she winked at him before leaving. He smiled.

"Wait". He called back to her. "Why are you leaving so fast?"

"I'm in a big time hurry".

"What sayest thou?" He questioned, pretending he did not hear what she just said. But in essence, he was trying to impress her with his knowledge of the terms of Christian book of faith.

"Big time hurry" she said, this time, a bit louder.

"That's understandable. Get in touch".

"Sure".

The woman visited a couple of other men for a good-time before she got home. One of the men made her laugh, treated her nice, and paid for a taxi-cab to take her home. Instead of going straight to her home, she veered off to the residence of another man.

But the second love was a spoiler. He figured out right away that she had given her show to another man before coming to him. He slapped her, and did not even kiss her goodbye. If she were his wife, the angry man would have killed her.

She left. Enraged. When she got home, she was ready to take it out on her own kid.

"It's because of you I suffer" she blamed it on her innocent kid who had no idea why and who slapped her.

"I've heard you say that before, mother. I don't know when you'll quit saying that" her child lamented. Protested.

"Cut it off crimp. I've warned you against talking back whenever I scold you. When I was your age, my mother used to spank me real good…"

"But you spanked me the other day. You're talking again about lack of moral value, teachers spanking you in schools, your dirty father and mother spanking you all the time. All your neighbors doing nothing but spanking you…" her kid was her equal in acid tongue.

"How dare you call my mother and father 'dirty' you scum. I did everything for you and all you're using to pay me back is to insult my parents". She cast a glance at her right hand side. Her eyes caught a deflated football which she bought for him a few months ago. She rushed to it, grabbed it, and threw it at him. The boy caught it in the mid-air, in a very athletic manner. He was pretty good in sports. Perhaps he thought he was going to have a ball. He threw it back at his mother. The ball hit her in the head, she yelled. He grinned.

She looked at him, offended at her son's victory. She frowned; then, she grimaced and then, she cursed him. "God will punish you".

"You too". The boy retorted.

"Me?"

"Yes".

"I warned you," she said and became very angry. She wanted to turn the house upside down, tear the boy into pieces. She darted her anger to look at him again, looked around, to find a better weapon with which to finish him off. Her eyes caught hold of another weapon. This time a set of silverware. She grabbed them, and threw the spoons, forks and knives at him. A couple of the knives tore through his shirt. A fork gave him a black-eye. And a spoon hit him on the temple, between the eyes.

The boy was enraged. Charged. And furious. He grimaced. His mother jumped around her kitchen searching for more weapons to finish up her battle.

CHAPTER EIGHTEEN (B)

Suddenly, the boy began to cry. Hardly had his tears rolled down his cheeks when his mother grabbed her best weapon, a handgun, to give her battle a finishing touch.

"Mommy cool, cool mommy. Please don't kill me. I will be nice next time".

"No way" she placed her final verdict. The boy was a condemned child, condemned to die at the hand of his own mother. She pulled the trigger, quick on it to blow her son's brain to River Jordan. The thing jammed. She looked, examined it. There was no bullet in the gun.

"Stay there scum. I'm coming back. I bore you in my womb. I had the right to abort you then. And I still have the right…" she groaned. She rushed through the stairs to her bedroom upstairs.

When she came down, the boy was nowhere to be found.

Two hours later, a line of armed police-men in their bullet proof vests drove by to her two storied house. She was still searching for her unaborted 'scum' when she heard the police siren loud and clear.

As the police force approached her house, it became clearer to her that her son had escaped, called the police on her. And that she had no option but to hide her last weapons.

She opened her six-round, fully loaded, Xino-made pistol. She began to combine removing the bullets from the pistol with rushing back through the stairs to hide them in her bedroom. However, both activities did not work well for her.

She mis-stepped on one of the stairs, and a couple of the bullets felled off from her land. As she tried to regain her stand, a sharp pain itched in her waist. She moaned. By this time, the policemen were at her door, banging at her door, and issuing their own command.

"Open the door. Police".

"Oh my God" she said to herself.

Suddenly, her waist pain disappeared. She stood up, picked up the fallen bullets, and shouted back at the cops at the door.

"Go away".

From the other side, a no-nonsense police sergeant who led the police squad showed off his power in a new way.

"Knock the door down" he ordered his Police Squad.

They did. The woman became hysterical. She pulled her dining table to block the men from entering. But two of the policemen had already made it inside her room.

She tried to re-load her gun. Speedily she succeeded. But before she could cork it to shoot, one of the policemen, good at karate, kicked the gun away from her hand. She ran into another room, and banged the door. Before the policemen were able to knock the second door open, she had already made her way to the back door.

Her house was big – The house she stole from Kukumba, that was, with the help of her lover, the Duke; the huge house and all the rooms in it were pretty confusingly elaborate, all credits due to her loot by deception. And each of the rooms offered a grand design in confusion, especially to anyone, for example, any intruder who had never lived in that very house before.

Her dog emerged from its hiding place, barked several times, and bit one of the cops. But another cop shot it dead. He did it with just one shot.

And one and nothing but one bullet silenced the attack dog. While she was opening her storm door to escape, a policeman grabbed her. She was just about to punch him when she saw a female cop who was pointing a police gun at her.

"Don't even think about it". Her match, the police-woman, commanded her.

Within a minute, she was hand-cuffed and her "rights" were read to her.

"You have a right to remain silent. Whatever you say can be a perfect excuse for your imprisonment…"

"I want to call my lawyer" she protested. "I have a right".

"Yes, not a "right" to kill your son". The police-woman talked back at her.

"He is not a son. He is a scum".

"Yes, and you are the mother of a scum. Let me tell you lady. Many women are out there who are praying to God to give them a baby half as smart as yours…"

"He is not a good boy. He is dumb, foolish, and I wish he were dead".

"You wish he were dead, huh?"

"I wouldn't miss him for a moment".

"He will soon be gone. He has already filled a suit to divorce you. I tried to discourage him. But now, I can see you are not fit to be a mother".

"To divorce me? My own child? I am not his wife. Am I?" her mood changed.

"That's what you get for being a Lousy mother. You nagged at him, humiliated him, and even tried to kill him. You are horrible I feel sorry for a man who will think of taking you for a wife".

"Not me". The police man who captured her in-toned.

"You see what I mean?". The police woman continued. "You are so bad that it shows. Who is the father of what unlucky child?".

"None of your damn business". She replied to the police woman.

"I know it is not. Who cares anyway? But sooner than later, you will need me. Don't forget what you've done. If I were you, I would listen to those who are trying to help, not show off my arrogance".

"What was your question?". The woman in hand-cuffs asked, tempting to mend face.

"Who is the father of your unlucky chap?"

"My so?"

"Yes, your son".

"My ex. My ex-husband". That in itself was not true. She had never been married. She had been playing a head-game with many men. And the boy, her son, was in truth a true blood of the ex-Governor.

"Are you divorced?".

"No, he committed suicide".

"You drove him to his death!" The police woman shouted at her. Then with a gentle voice as if in a whisper, she put it to her, to drive her point home. "Didn't you?"

"No. He was no good". Her defiance, up again.

"Like his son?"

"Yes"

"I see. You killed him, and now you want to kill his son. What an awful woman". She jeered at her. Having jeered at her, she, the police woman, began to laugh at her.

Here was a woman whose parents wanted to become a lawyer. Here she stood, talking, arguing, and questioning like a trained lawyer, and daily, putting her very life in harm's way.

Her father had all the money she needed to go to college and law school to study law. But she flatly refused, preferring to fight crimes with force.

From the day she saw a television advertisement – showing how young women, fresh out of high schools could do a fine job in the police force, she decided, that to be her calling. Of course, she joined the police force barely two days after graduation from high school. Her father, a college professor, tried in vain to reason with her.

CHAPTER EIGHTEEN (C).

This was her third year in the armed police force. She had been decorated many times, after having a close-call to death in five different instances. In each of those instances, a police life was taken, every one of them, her partner in duty.

She made it clear to all her partners, during a tough assignment, to never reveal what they would be going through to her parents. In fact, her parents were never told about the instances that their daughter walked through the shadows of near-death. She had seen tough times in action. She had played it rough; seen blood, and taken the lives of, at least, thirty-five hardcore criminals in all, while fighting to neutralize them.

She was happy with her job, her life, and with all intrigues, excitements, terrible dangers, and joy of victories that her challenging job held in store for her.

It was time to reveal their new conquest. This one, the camera men would praise them. She knew it. And her male partner was proud, too.

Meanwhile, all the other members of the police squad were still searching the big house, not knowing that the woman had been captured. It was already fifteen minutes ever since they stormed the big house with the squad leader having nothing to show for it.

On their way to the suspect's residence, it was his considered opinion that this job would take him and his Police Squad five minutes. He even said it to his squad, hoping to do other things after her apprehension.

By this time, fifteen minutes on a minor exercise, was, to him, too much. He became very impatient. His squad officers were having a thorough search of the house…This was so, because the numerous rooms in the big house, coupled with the way the house was built, made it more unfamiliar, even difficult, especially for these cops, who were, no doubt, a set of unfamiliar hands.

The sergeant had called for three consecutive times earlier, by his walkie-talkie, to enquire whether his squad had come up with something. Their response in each of those earlier calls was:

"No Serg".

The fourth time, the squad leader called:

"Caught her yet?" He was a man of action. He left his police cruiser, its sophisticated radio-telephone-gizmo, and went straight to lead the operation, the moment he arrived at the destination. He liked to stand by his squad, as an able leader, while they did their job. To him, performance was the spirit of police-man-ship.

"Roja, Serg. You got it".

The woman in uniform stood to bring out her own walkie-talkie. But before she could reach it, she heard that said by her male partner.

Earlier, she was leaning, like a lawyer toward their capture, the "awful" woman.

"Fine". She could hear from her boss, the superior police sergeant's response through the walkie-talkie.

When Miss Ruby Dolgman joined the police force, her passion was to perform up to par among her male counterparts. It was because of this passion that made her to insist on participating in any duty which demanded tough, rough, and ready response.

Her territorial boss, Sergeant Cigarmania held her in high regard. And despite the way he admired her courage, he harbored a secret concern for her safety, since she was a woman – As such, he felt that she should be protected by a man.

Sergeant Cigarmania was a tough cop – A stone-faced individual whose enigmatic facial expression would hardly reveal his inner feelings.

"Ruby" he said "You and Corporal Jack Festa have done a good job"

"Just doing our job, boss" she responded.

"I'm sure everyone at the H.Q. will be pleased"

"Thanks Serg." she replied. And her counterpart, Corporal Jack Festa, smiled the way he did when Ruby lashed out at the amusing phase of her interrogation of the suspect.

"Are you always this way?" Ruby asked Jack. No doubt, she liked him and he liked her too. Somehow they managed to keep their professional distance, lest one accuse the other of unprofessional behavior.

CHAPTER NINETEEN

The dancers were ready. So ready that it showed. Prince Kingsley had not known there existed a place, where keen believers and pagans worshipped together on their individual schedules. It was an ecumenical in its highest order.

It was an eye-opening experience, an awareness in an ace of revelation. It all began in a carriage bus. Kingsley, no longer a royal trainee nor a captive, but a factory worker – was on his own way from work to one of the remaining chained forests, which he chose for his residence. He had vowed never again to live in a better place till the native people began to receive an equal treatment to that received always by the descendants of the conquistadors.

It just happened, as events often did, a bald-headed old fellow was making a pass at a young woman. A razor-sharp tongued woman, she did not hesitate to let him know how she felt – and where he belonged.

"Get your hands off me, you sleazy old dog".

To everybody's surprise, the 'sleazy old dog' smiled and gave her a captivating wonder.

"I'm not what you think. I'm a sexy, rich senior citizen".

"No, you're not" responded the young woman. Indeed, she contradicted him.

"My sweet damsel, the melody of your voice is pure melody to my dancing soul" said the old man.

"Wait a minute. Did you just call me a damsel when I threw a dirty load of insult at you?"

"My dear, what my soul heard is remarkably different from what you think you said" said the old man. And the tone of voice, this time, truly changed her. His words radically converted her. For example, her former temper-laden face became a new face rich in contagious smile. His wonder-working words did uncommon wonder on her heart, and they diluted, rather changed her acid tongue to a lovely thing. Then, the way she responded to his next charming words, made her a new woman. She became mellow in words and in her actions.

"What a man. All your four hundred wives must be the happiest women in the whole world" she responded. Her words were so mellow and so cordial and so inviting.

"Common, I'm rich; my Mercedes 450 SE is parked by the bus station. You're free to join me. We can take a spin".

Are you serious?"

You'll see. I'm a free spirit. A man is as old as he feels".

"You're damn right" she agreed. More agreeable. "You better be rich, otherwise, I will shoot you" she said, smiling. She was a woman, a free spirit, too. Everyone was looking for fame and fortune. They could come anytime and anywhere, when the one in search least expected them. They were the things that made for a good time. She was a citizen of a New Kingdom where every woman was an ardent seeker of love, fortune and fame.

The women here did not hide their feelings like the 'primitive natives'. They really wanted the men's wealth; and they were after what men had got, and they would tell the men so. You had money, they were there for you. You did not, then you had to spend your miserable nights alone. It was that simple. They were liberated women – Liberated in every way.

When a man did not satisfy a woman, she would dump him and tell him, "God bless, goodbye. It's over". And that was it. The man would have to start all over, while the woman would lose only him. The man would lose all his belongings, while the woman would be at the receiving end of those belongings.

Beside, Kingsley saw another fellow talking with a woman old enough to be his mother. He had an artificial band of moustache on to conceal his youthful appearance.

He touched her gently. She smiled readily almost as if they were getting ready to go to bed. In the olden days, when the Kingdom was purely Olarkwudo, no one would have seen such an exchange between a mere boy and his elder, a woman. But the people were not even advanced enough to invent something substantial; speak less about coming up with this kind of luxurious bus which they themselves were calling "prostitutes paradise".

Anyway, the boy told her more and more sweet things – The things she would love to hear. He was there telling her those little lies that men often told the love-struck women – which such women often believed men. He told her what a great guy he was. She believed him with her whole heart. He added that he was a son of a millionaire. She believed that too.

While those things were going on, the luxurious bus was cruising along. It was a state-of-the art luxury bus. Poor folks such as most of the natives could not afford to board it. The fare was expensive – too expensive for them. A native working at his harsh, low-paying job, would have used all his three weeks' earnings to board the bus for just an hour. To him, that was a wrong idea; economically, a wrong proposition.

CHAPTER NINETEEN (B)

The young-man's and older-woman's conversation changed dramatically into a different phase. Kingsley was watching them, when, all of a sudden, the old woman stared squarely in the boy's face. It seemed she had no shame. Her desire was intense. It seemed she would kill if her prospect did not read her mind perfectly and act accordingly on it.

She needed the boy just at least to touch her again. She was surely what the people called 'a passion flower' that bloomed instantly at the very touch of the handsome boy. Her stare turned into a broad smile as soon as the boy did exactly what she wanted: It was a kiss. And it pleased her immensely.

"Please hold my hand" she gave her hand to him.

"Sure" said the lad. He took her hand and held it.

Again she needed something. She stared and got it. This time it was a hug. She leaned on him a bit longer than was normal. The boy savored every moment of it.

"You said your dad is rich, didn't ya?"

"Sure, he is".

"What are you going to do with all that money when he dies?"

"I figure I'm going to have a ball" answered the lad. And the way he said it, it sounded as if he wished he had a very rich father who would leave him with a huge inheritance.

"I know what you can do" said the old woman.

"Tell me. I'll be pleased to hear it from you".

"You buy me a Volvo; buy a huge house where you and I would live ever after" she said. First, she began to point to him her own needs. Then she added, "Of course you can invest some of those money wisely so we won't have to run out of residual income".

"That's a good idea. I've not thought of that". He held her closer, even tightly so. She stared again. This time, she stared in a way that reflected her new mood – To drag him into the bed of the dream house.

CHAPTER NINETEEN (C)

The old man and his new love did not give up. In fact, they were becoming intensely more acquainted than ever. She would hold her hand across his shoulder. In turn, he would touch her wherever he wanted. In short, they were not only enjoying each other by now, they were having a good time as well.

Hardly had the "prostitutes' paradise" stopped when the newly-made friends were hand-in-hand, walking off the luxurious bus. As they made their way to the exit/entrance stairs of the bus, her step slipped.

"Oh" she said. But it was a trick; the experienced old man knew it. And he knew what to do in such an 'accident' – To help the victim.

He reached out and helped her stand.

"Thank you" she said. Then, she added, "You are sweet".

"You are highly welcome" the old man relished her 'thank you'.

He held her closer; which she needed as they walked away.

"Look. See over there". The man pointed.

"IS that yours?"

"Well, it can be yours as well. I've got an ocean-going liner plying down the Pacific through the Indian Ocean. My new yatch is anchored by the river, a couple of miles from here…" the love hungry 'sleazy old dog' started adding one attractive sale's pitch after another. He did not finish presenting all his baits when 'his fish' dived in for it.

"Are you married?" she asked. Eagerly. She was available. She wouldn't resist if the 'sexy, rich, senior citizen' would be kind enough to claim her.

"I was. But she left me for a younger man".

"Oh-h poor thing". However, the way she said 'poor thing' was not convincing. In fact, the man knew it. She was secretly happy, hoping she would ably utilize this very heaven-sent opportunity; use this opportunity to impress the man well enough to have him accept her into the vacuum created by his ex-love.

"Yeah, I know" answered the old man.

"Was she pretty?" she asked him.

"Beauty lies on the eyes of the beholder". The man was smart. He knocked her beauty-question with a popular quotation. This rich man, she thought, must be so experienced that he could not be fooled by physical attraction. She was not lacking in intelligence and some earned experience either. So, she reasoned, the best way to go was to switch to a better tactic.

"Were there any misunderstanding? I mean, I mean…" she couldn't finish her lines when the 'sleazy old dog' came to her rescue.

"There is always a room for disagreement in a relationship. Well, she was a pretty good woman. The trouble was, I guess, I didn't have what she wanted…"

She saw her opportunity; not to be an advocate, because that would ruin her chance. Not to take the side of his ex, because that would jeopardize their new relationship. But to play a role of an outsider who would be ready to switch to his side, was a sure bet to win him.

"What could that be?" she asked him, measuring the tone of every word, its inflection and its pitch.

"Youthful appearance".

"That's odd. I thought you had an argument or something or a fight. Tell me, did you ever argue with her?"

"Yes, of course".

"Did you beat her up?"

"Hell no. I am not that kind of man. I will never raise my hand against a woman. My father did that, and it resulted to the death of my mother. He regretted it till he died. I'm old enough to learn from the mistakes of others".

"I'm sorry to hear that" she consoled him. The man brought out a handkerchief. She took it from him and used it to wipe out his tears. The question, of course, touched his most sensitive nerve.

"It's so hard. Life is not fair"

"Please, let's talk about this some other time" she tried to terminate the conversation.

"No, please. No, no, please". He encouraged her to continue with the conversation.

"Did she cheat on you? I'm sorry, I know this is a silly question" she quickly apologized to him.

"No, and, yes, she had flings with youths of her own age, several times till I couldn't take it anymore".

CHAPTER TWENTY

It was not until one year later when Kingsley saw them again. This time, they were happily married. And not only were they happily married, their beautiful marriage was greatly blessed with a very handsome kid.

They were fast. She secured her position in his life, very fast. Luckily for her, her first child to him was a boy, the very thing the man greatly wanted. To him, the boy was god-sent.

He married Ezialor hoping she would make it. But she left him, an impotent lady who was not ashamed of her barrenness.

"Excuse me sir, didn't we meet in a 'Prostitutes' Paradise sometime last year…?"

"Oh yes, son. It was the day I met my wife" he answered. Then, he touched her. She drew closer to him. Their baby was in her hands.

"I thought…" said Prince Kingsley.

"…Don't think son. It's the 'sleazy old dog'. She was right"

"He is a very understanding man. I'm so proud of him" she added. Her eyes, fixed at Kingsley.

"This is my son". He proudly interrupted.

"Our baby. Say hi to him". She held up her son's hand in a greeting gesture. Kingsley held his hand, the baby smiled.

"Say hi, honey, will you?" The dad added, somewhat in a commanding tone. All of them smiled. The man was as robust as he was when their paths crossed a year earlier. This time though, he was sleek, and bursting with more enthusiasm. His wife was more gorgeous now. Having enjoyed some quantities of the sexy, rich senior citizen's riches, she was reflecting, and they showed.

"He will grow up to be a great man" said Kingsley.

"You think so?" The lady with baby asked.

"Sure he will. It is in the blood. His grand dad was great. His father is great. He will be great too". Without giving any of them room to dispute him, he went ahead and told Kinsley one of the exciting hide-outs he used to visit, after his first wife left him. And he advised Kingsley to check it out.

When Kingsley visited the Universal Ecumenical Church, he did it out of curiosity. He had heard that some believers and non-believers were having affairs in the holy, high place; but he did not have the slightest inkling that such things could be happening inside the holy house where the Supreme Being was supposed to be worshipped.

At the first gate was a revealing message inscribed for all to read:

"Come and worship him"

Then, the second gate was a massage that shocked everyone that passed through the first gate for the first time:

"To the Devil the glory be".

Prince Kingsley entered into the holy house. And he looked inside. Lo and behold there were many people, at least, ten scores and two. They were busy, doing some holy rituals. And while they were doing their rituals, more and more people came in. And before the end of the rituals, which, obviously were Satanic ceremonies, the people in attendance were more than a couple of gross in number.

Right after the gate was a table manned by a young lady and a handsome man, both in their early thirties. As Kingsley gathered the information letter, this place was an assembly of an exclusive cult, the inner-circle of the Devil's worshippers.

Surprisingly, the people who belonged to this cult body were some of the richest people in the New Kingdom.

The young man and the young woman were the entrance fee collectors. The amount per head was sound enough to feed a homeless, primitive native two square meals for five complete days. But these people were more eager to pay and enter than to think about the homeless issue which had no bearing in their lives.

He stood before them, calm, regal, ramrod and imperial. It was just like a case of a tropical yam saying to its harvester:

"Dig deep because I have a mighty tuber".

CHAPTER TWENTY (B)

When Kingsley presented himself to the entrance 'tickets' sellers, before they could open up their mouths, to tell him how much a ticket was, he brought out some currency bills, and gave the money to them.

"This is too much." The young lady said.

"I know" replied Kingsley. "Five is for you; five for this guy beside you; and five for me".

"All right" the male entrance fee collector replied in proud jubilation.

"There is still some change sir" the young woman indicated.

"Please use it for other two people who might have no money for their tickets" responded Prince Kingsley. Then, he moved regally; his shoulders held truly regally high as he moved into the magnificent hall.

When Kingsley entered deep into the splendid sanctuary the two impressed fee collectors began to talk about him.

"He must be super-rich where he came from" the man said to his bill-collecting partner.

"I shall marry him" The lady replied.

"Are you falling in love with a total stranger…?"

"I don't care. He's cute".

The Prince was in the midst of decaying civilization. He looked around. The impression and indeed what he saw was an ominous evidence that the New Kingdom was on a path of no return.

The empire in question rose at a time in-between the reign of Ottoman, the religious guru of a certain empire. And that, in a far, far-away land. Perhaps this empire learnt something from the zealot.

The unholy enclave was a far cry from what the New Kingdom constantly told the whole world that it stood for. For example, the New Kingdom was so independent in the spirit of killing the weak natives of the land.

It was a sobering delight for the Prince. Sobering, in that the moral value which this Great Kingdom proclaimed, so loud overseas, as its beacon of principle, was woefully lacking here. A delight because the peoples' patience chilled out the contradictions; and as they did, their hearts simply went cold. Though their patience was ironic as physical proposition, it was out of control in terms of spiritual proportion.

The exposure in this arena was an exposure to a new challenge; a dare to challenge and risk to die. The Prince had not forgotten his days in the dungeon, the war his people fought, and the struggles ahead. The war was a challenging endeavor. His brave people fought with valor, but it was a lost cause. His chosen home, the chained forest, was a perpetual reminder that things were not the way that his own father wanted them to be. For example, in the chained forest, making a living was, in good measure, a practical demonstration of the idea of the survival of the strongest for most of the people – Surely for the natives.

At one end of the sanctuary were the naked dancers in the house of the 'New Lord' of the Kingdom. They performed their rituals in a way that, if Jesus Christ was in the world in their days, he would have fought them off with either a sword or, with a gun instead of with a whip-cord.

In this place, the people were devoutly dancing to the devil. There was a reckless disregard for anything divine. One of the naked dancers shouted to Kingsley's horror:

"Praise be to the Devil". And to his greatest horror was how almost everyone in the great sanctuary responded:

"May his name be praised".

They jumped around, performed more rituals, and glorified their praises to the evil spirit they worshipped.

In fairness to morality, a novice witnessing this event would not help but see a world of contrast. Here was a Kingdom whose Duke's Order of Travelling Teachers had sent a message far and wide. A message which they wanted the world to hear. A message that this New Kingdom was built on the principles of **"Pure God. Pure Morality. And Pure Faith"**.

"O.P.P." One of the naked dancers shouted at Kingsley. But he acted as if he did not hear her. Again, she came closer to him and called him "O.P.P." giggling as she danced away. There were some music played at intervals. Each music was danceable. The atmosphere was great and inviting. Kingsley could not long endure before he joined the crowd in the dancing.

In the middle of the event, the young lady came to him, once again, and put her mouth very close to his ear and said "O.P.P." The Prince was irritated. At the end of that very record, a pop music for sure, three young men came to him. Each of them offered a hand in turn for a hand-shake. Kingsley obliged. And they left. Friendly, they were.

About five minutes after they left, they came back to where he stood with cans of beer. But Kingsley refused on the ground that "I do not drink alcohol; thank you anyway".

As they left, the young woman who called him O.P.P. approached him, yet again. This time she was dressed up in a stunning outfit. Beside her was a young-man, somewhat younger than she was.

"O.P.P. this is my brother, Kubi" she introduced her brother to the Prince.

"Well, would you, if you wouldn't mind, tell me what O.P.P. means?" Kingsley asked.

"Up and down; that's O.P.P." she answered.

Kingsley wrote them down on a piece of paper, "O.P.P." and 'up and down' "Well, O.P.P. is not an acronym for 'up and down', is it?" Kingsley asked her.

"Yes, O.P.P. is up and down" she answered.

One thing Kingsley failed to understand, however, was that the one who repeatedly called him O.P.P. was an aggressive egg. Women here were remarkably different from menfolk. Oftentimes, they sent out their own signals to the men they liked in diverse ways. For example, an aggressive egg whose desire it was to enjoy a romantic moment with a chosen man, would go ahead to criticize before him, all the homosexual men that she had met. By so doing, she challenged him to prove to her his own non-homosexual manhood.

It was many a code so subtle…a clue many men often failed to decode the signals…And whenever a woman did offer herself to a man…It was another thing altogether for a very discerning man to grab the woman; howbeit, accept her offer for a romantic engagement.

Women in the New Kingdom talked a lot about the men in their lives, the men of their dream, the ones they desired to have, and the ones they plainly liked. A dream man was an enduring thing for conversation of every living woman. This very conversation was always the women's favorite, and typical. And it always went on, especially, when the choice man was not around.

CHAPTER TWENTY (C)

When Kubi's sister went so far to draw the attention of Prince Kingsley, she did so based on her cultural conditioning. Nevertheless, all that she wanted the O.P.P. to do was to prove to her, how-so-ever, in his own way, to justify his manhood. Kingsley was not experienced; a novice so naïve that he failed her simple test, many times. She looked at him, her earlier smiles were no longer there. Perhaps she was either deeply saddened, or furiously disappointed in him. Either way, she did neither show a temper nor voice her feelings out. Possibly she viewed his lack of perception and insensitivity to her cues as a pure reflection of a man whose state of affair was nothing but a pure basket case.

Kingsley hardly tried to read new meaning into her presence. This was firmly reinforced, again and again with his inability to read her face and study her mind. She was a woman. And she needed to protect her pride, especially in the presence of her own brother. One would have understood that.

Since she was with her own brother, she did not have to create the impression as a flirt, even though she had been. For sure, her brother would not have appreciated that…unless they were the other way – The people of incest. Her baits were enough to entice a hungry fish. Kingsley seemed like a hungry-less fish. If not so, at least his reaction gave the impression.

Again, Kingsley naively walked the other track of her mind. The wrong one. He tried to argue with her. Hopeless. Then, tempted to lecture her on the difference between O.P.P. and up and down. All these efforts were all in vain.

"I can't help you". Kingsley blurted out in anger.

"Oh yeah? Even if you saw a lady in danger, you would be so self-centered as to not reach out and help. Is that what you are telling me?" asked Kubi's sister.

"We are not in a forest. There are no lions and tigers threatening to harm you. I do not understand where you are heading with all these" said Prince Kingsley.

"Oh yeah?" asked Kubi's sister.

"Yes, by the way my name is not O.P.P. Please next time call me Kingsley". And he began to walk away.

"Kingsley" the other fellow with her shouted. Kingsley turned and smiled.

"Bye" Kingsley waved at them.

CHAPTER TWENTY-ONE

A few steps away was a glowing electric signal post with these words: "Entrance only". It was a very enticing electrical light fixture; exuding a romantic blend of red, green and blue light rays in an alternate fashion.

Kingsley liked such a thing. He went straight ahead.

"Kingsley" Someone called him. He looked. Behold, a good friend of his, the 'sleazy old dog' he met in the exclusive transport bus.

"I am so glad to see you again" Kingsley stretched out his right hand. They bowed before each other, and shook each other's hand. He knew Kingsley was royal.

"Great place; isn't it?" the older man observed.

"It is wonderful. It seems there is a wealth of entertainment going on here" Kingsley put in.

"Follow me. Son, see. Beneath the stairways is a world of contrast. Follow me. Son, just follow me". He led the way, Kingsley followed.

Beneath the stairs was a paved hall-way that led to the basement of this church building. The basement was much different from the sanctuary on top. Here was a state-of-the-art architectural masterpiece known as "The Worshippers' Rostrum". Here too, people of variable sexual persuasion, were unanimously bound, in mutual agreement, to practice their sexual preferences without interference, whatsoever.

Kingsley hardly knew what awaited his eyes when the friend, who he knew, called him, and beckoned him to the under-ground Rostrum.

At one corner of the Rostrum, he saw a couple of naked women misbehaving. Kingsley turned his eyes away, acting as if he saw nothing. As he ventured to walk away,

"Hey" he heard. He turned to look.

"Shame on you". One of the two misbehaving women hauled at him.

"Please I didn't see anything" Kingsley apologized.

"You saw everything". The second woman retorted.

"Come and join us". The first woman requested.

"No, thanks"

"I wasn't serious. Fool".

"I've got to go". Kingsley was about to excuse himself from them.

"Shame! Shame! Shame!" The two women simultaneously hauled at him, pointing and clinching their fists; they began to walk towards him in a way that spelt out nothing but trouble. Kingsley saw them coming; hastily, he disappeared out of their sight, as he mingled away into the crowd.

"Why did you stop to look?" his older friend questioned him in a tense rebuke.

"I didn't know…"

"They have their guns, they could kill, Kingsley, any intruder, Kingsley".

"They have no right…" Kingsley was about to argue.

"They have every right in the book. This is their land".

"No, it's not. They stole it from the natives".

"That is rubbish. The land is theirs. It doesn't matter how they acquired it" said the older man.

"But I believe the land is not rightfully theirs" Kingsley disagreed.

"Right is what a man writes on a piece of paper. Right is what you have on your young mind. But right on paper or right on your mind is no right at all. A man with a might is a man that is right" said the older man.

"Illuminating. Where did you get such crazy ideas?" asked Kingsley.

"From your crazy head" replied the older man.

"I am sorry. I did not mean to be disrespectful to my elder" said Prince Kingsley remorsefully.

"You are young. Sometimes the youths get carried away with their ideas about what is morally right or wrong in our Great Society" said the older man.

Hardly had they finished their argument, when they saw a group of people offering some animal sacrifice. A goat and rooster were slaughtered.

There was an altar at the center of the Rostrum. This altar was decorated with colorful pictures. Directly above the altar were chandeliers of assorted colors. All the seven colors of a rainbow were neatly represented on the light fixtures on the ceiling.

There were twinkling light rays emitting from the chandeliers' miniature light bulbs. Others were either less brightly colored. Intermediate, or more dazzling than the others. A globe-like light fixture was located at the center of the chandeliers. This one was rotating and exuding its own moon-like but spotted rays to the whole blend of colors. The whole blend of colors was so beautiful. And the total combination was something with a special effect. There was a special hue, serenity and wonderful delight.

The whole thing was tantalizing. Kingsley could not resist. The sight was alluring. He drew nearer. This time, he could see the objects of sacrifice clearer. Beside the two sacrificial ones, which he saw, was a pig tied to a pillar. A few steps away from the pig was another object for sacrifice – This one, a man. He was solidly chained to one of the tall brick columns that held the entire church building, rostrum and all.

The man, sacrificial one, was a native, an ex-warrior, turned a slave in the conquered land.. When Kingsley saw him, his predicament, he visualized the horrors awaiting the man.

"This is wrong" Kingsley shouted, his finger pointing at the helpless man chained to the pillar.

"I know, but what can you do?" His friend agreed, but with a note of resignation.

"Let's call the cops at once" insisted Kingsley.

"If we try, they will know. The law is behind them. I think many of the people around here" Kingsley's friend, the watchful 'sleazy old dog' looked around to support his argument, "Are members of the police force".

"This is sacrilegious. I can't stand it" said Prince Kingsley.

"If you try, Kingsley, they will know. And they gonna kill you. I've seen this before; better save your neck".

"It's better I die saving that poor man than see his throat slashed for a bloody sacrifice. He is no goat. Off I go" responded Prince Kingsley. And he took off.

CHAPTER TWENTY-ONE (B).

Two days later, two government officials appeared at Kingsley's door with a warrant to arrest and deport him. They were immigration police officers. When they knocked, Kingsley answered.

"Are you Kingsley?" one of the two men asked.

"Yes, I am"

"You are under arrest"

"What for?"

"For civil violation, disruption of religious liberty, and disturbance of peace". The police officer charged; the shorter one added, so that he would know how terrible the crimes he committed were:

"As an alien in our land, common sense should have told you respect for the Supreme One is something even a child knows is pretty sacred".

"That's absurd. They wanted to kill a man and I stopped them. If that is all you've just charged, then I am guilty. You can deport me to wherever you like. But if saving the life of someone in danger is a genuine respect for the law, and a civil obligation, then you are at liberty to arrest those wicked men who were truly breaking the law" Kingsley narrated.

"Wait a moment; are you saying that those guys were trying to kill someone?" The other officer, the taller one, asked.

"Exactly".

"Can you prove it?" The first officer added with some air of disdain.

"I have all the evidence in the book, in the world to substantiate my claim".

"Well, it sounds like someone is telling lies somewhere" the other officer who said 'wait a minute…' added.

"I know" Kingsley agreed. "And it is those people".

"Well, you will have to follow us to the police station to tell the Chief all that you saw. No need to put a handcuff on you. We'll give every protection you need just in case those guys try to get even with you".

"I don't care whether I die in the process or not; I am convinced that killing your fellow human being for a sacrifice is wrong. I am persuaded…"

"Please don't sermonize. You sound like a preacher…" the short officer who wanted to arrest him interrupted.

"Shut up. The guy is true to his faith. I will not stand here and allow you to interrupt a witness who is determined to expose a horrible crime he witnessed" the second immigration officer rushed in to the rescue.

"I know you hate me" the short officer challenged the tall one.

"I do not. But I hate your reasoning faculty because you reason like a pig" the tall officer explained.

"Yes, yes, there was also a pig there". The 'pig' the officer mentioned helped Kingsley to remember the pig he saw in the church's Rostrum.

"Where?" The officer who defended Kingsley asked him.

"In the Rostrum, below the church hall" replied Kingsley. The short officer burst into a laughter.

"Why are you laughing?" he was asked by his coadjutor.

"The witness is a liar. What a ludicrous allegation" the other officer explained.

"Sir, with all due respect, I am not lying. I will appreciate it if you will respect me and not laugh at me when I speak the truth" Kingsley stated, and that with a subdued rage.

"Who are you to tell me what to do?" the short angry officer questioned. But Kingsley ignored his question.

"Enough" the other officer barked.

CHAPTER TWENTY-TWO

"How many times will a man slay a tiger before he would be called a tiger-slayer?"

"I think once".

"Good. Once you've done something, there is no erasing the ink".

"I am beginning to understand".

"If you have enough common-sense, which I believe you do" he paused "you have captured the whole message".

"I think I get your message".

"Don't just say you think". The man commanded. "Tell me you've captured the entire message".

"As your soul lives, may the Great Spirit be my witness, that's fine. Your words are clear to me as the bright sun of the day".

"You are a son of the soil. I am getting old. You have punched a hole in the crime of the wicked. The new Governor will see what his people have been doing in the name of religion. Is freedom to sacrifice the weak a religious freedom?" The old man stared at him for an answer.

"No, it is not"

"May the Great Spirit honor you for speaking the living truth. May the wicked never live to see the day the Great Spirit would honor you. Moreover, may the Great Spirit stand in the way of anyone who would dare to stand in the way of the truth. And I say: May the Great Spirit curse those who twist the living truth for their selfish gain" said the old man.

"Yes, that is how it is. Before they came, our people used to use fruits of the land for sacrifice. But they called it primitive. When they use their enemies as burnt offerings, they call it civilization". Kingsley replied.

"I have prayed to the extent that heaven and earth themselves can bear witness that I have prayed". The Sage who visited Kingsley to praise him for exposing the human sacrifices declared.

"Why?" Kingsley asked.

"Why?" the seemingly confused Sage said back to him.

"Yes, why, our father?" asked Kingsley.

"You mean why have I prayed?" the Sage wanted to understand what Kingsley was asking about.

"No".

"No? What then do you mean?" asked the wise Sage.

"Well, why are your prayers not answered?"

"Ask the Great Spirit. Ask their God. By the way, say God backwards".

"I can't say that". Kingsley refused to obey him.

"Yes, you can do it. Say God backwards for me".

"He may get angry at me if I say that". Kingsley gave a reason.

"If he kills you, you endure it. After all, we've seen more dead not to be afraid of dying. Say 'God' backward for me". The visiting Sage insisted.

"Dog" Prince Kingsley said pretty reluctantly.

"That's correct. Their God is their dog. He defends them and attacks their enemies" said the wise Sage.

"You are indeed a Sage. You see through the enchanted smoke-ball" said Prince Kingsley.

The sage smiled. His broad-grinning face changed suddenly to a facial expression full of seriousness.

"Prince. I shall always call you the Prince till I die. Listen to me very carefully". As the Sage said so, the Prince leaned towards him, gazing at him in rapt attention. The Sage saw that the young

Prince was fully ready for his words. He did not want him to miss a word of what he was about to say. He adjusted his seat.

"Our father, I am listening" said Prince Kingsley.

"Our future now lies in our hands. It is in the hands of young men like you. We should no longer be begging the powers of the sky to help us when they have already betrayed us in the past. Our cause was just. We did not ask for the war. The war came to us. We had to defend ourselves. But our gods deserted us at our supreme moments of horror and indescribable pain. We cannot blame ourselves for the mistakes of history. We did our best, but our best was not enough to protect us from our more powerful enemies" said the wise Sage.

The invaders from the North were many. Like the swarms of locusts they came, the heavenly warriors they invaded. They came killing both lives and live-stocks.

Everything in their way was subject to death. They had the means and the men to execute their war games.

They armed themselves to the teeth. In circumstances where some of their kit-and-kin-warriors were deprived, their psychology and charming manners completely disarmed those who they would have killed, were they in their shoes.

CHAPTER TWENTY-TWO (B)

It was the second time that the young-man and the middle-aged woman went out on a date. She smiled and radiated warmth at every moment the young man talked or smiled. She made him feel comfortable being with her. And she created the impression that she was so happy being with him.

The beautiful lady was once married. And her daughter was married to a young, native man. Despite her royal heritage, a 'Von' of noble parentage, she lent her whole-hearted support to her daughter's marriage, not minding that her own relatives frowned at the whole arrangement.

Since Kingsley brought the activities at the Universal Ecumenical church to the public, she could no longer help but fall in love with him. In the land, Prince Kingsley was a new hero of the people. And such a fact of life made him a man who was also hated by so many.

True heroes were so few in the land. And Prince Kingsley was one of the rarest heroes. This woman, one of the souls who loved to worship true heroes, she truly loved Prince Kingsley with consuming passion.

She was once a lover of the great merchant – The man who spent a lion-share of his fortune for the cause that he believed in…This woman was just like that, adoring those who challenged the authorities to bring about the needed changes in the vast land.

The young man, Kingsley, knew what he wanted in a woman. Though this one was much older, at least, ten years older, he intimated that he did not care about it. Her age, for sure.

"How old are you?" she asked him on their second date.

"Age is just a number. I don't know". Prince Kingsley answered.

"I like that" she replied, smiling.

At a point, they sat by a train-station, waiting for a train, just to cruise around. Trains and rail-roads were some of the civilizations the conquerors brought into the land. They were so many trains, and the train-lines crisscrossed the entire Kingdom.

The couple had no place in mind. However, they just wanted to board a train and go. Meanwhile, while the train tarried, they decided to play it by ear; this, with regard to where they would go. She was taller, much taller too. She, six feet and five inches. He, only five feet. His head could barely make it to her shoulder when they stood closer, side by side.

"I am old fashioned" she intimated.

It seemed to Kingsley, she was self-conscious. And indeed her self-consciousness was becoming more and more evident. She was conscious of her age, wondering whether he would dump her because of it. She did not feel this way during her three months' romance with the merchant, because he was her senior and much older.

Now she indicated her fear of what the New Kingdom called "date rape". Her fear was followed by a desire for what the same society referred to as "date respect".

Her mind was working faster. She pictured herself in the arms of this young man, the new hero. The new love, then she snapped from it. She remembered the first date she had with a prominent psycho-the-rapist; a man she later testified against in Court of the Law as 'psycho, the great rapist". It was a pathetic case. It was indeed the case that every self-respecting woman, in that type of situation, would not like it to be repeated. Yes, it was truly an experience that made her to become pretty distrustful of so many men.

But, in this case, here was a young man who had all the potentials to rule a kingdom.

"Perhaps he won't do it" she said to herself. Kingsley looked away, pretending he heard none of the two comments; 'I am old fashioned' and 'Perhaps he won't do it'.

"Von, the train is coming" said Prince Kingsley, pointing towards the east side of the rail-road. She liked the way he addressed her. It made her feel pretty royal, feel good, and feel better about herself. After all, she had a royal blood, though less direct to the crown than this young man did. Nevertheless, it was still royal blood, and something to be proud of. She returned his observation with a smile.

"Yes", she looked up eastwards "Isn't that exciting?"

"We're going to cruise around the city from one train station to another. We'll do so till we find another excitement".

"That would be lovely" she agreed, readily.

"Pee-ep". The blowing train's horn echoed around the train station. While the horn was still blowing, the passengers' train arrived at the train station.

Quickly, the train's sliding doors opened. Some passengers who had arrived at their destination came out. Kingsley and the woman plus other passengers who were waiting to board the train, stepped inside. Some of them sat on the vacant seats. Some, however, preferred to stand up. Those who stood up held their hands to the few frame-like poles, serving as structural supports to, by each of the coach's seat.

Kingsley and the woman sat close by each other.

"I just wanna thank you for the flowers you gave…"

"Oh, that was just a small thing" Prince Kingsley responded with an air of pride.

"It was so lovely to see the gentleman from the flower-shop" she said.

"Did you like the note attached to the flower?" asked Prince Kingsley..

"That was so nutty" she continued, her face and her mouth full of smiles.

"I am glad. Did they render an excellent service?" Kingsley asked, thus, showing her that he was a man that demanded nothing less than a perfect service.

"Yeah, the gentleman was in tuxedo, all dressed up, clean-shaven, handsome, oh".

"You loved the…"

"It was a neat package. It was so lovely. Thank you so…"

"You are welcome".

CHAPTER TWENTY-THREE

The Center for inter-Religious Worships was a grand design in architectural structure of its kind. It was popularly called: "The Universal Ecumenical Church.

There were four entrances to this building. And each way was located half-way, each side, of the oblong-shaped church building.

On Monday nights, the people whose method of worship was in harmony with the *'primitive native religion'*, came in and did their service. On this day, a self-styled Sacramentarian would administer to his group, the religious sacraments. One would see him lead the group in chanting rituals; and induced masturbation was practiced among them.

In addition, passing around of some rolled up sticks of marijuana was part of the whole deal. The members would put flaming lights on the one-end of each of the dried, rolled-up "weeds". By inhaling the smoke of the marijuana, they believed, their dead ancestors would reveal the dual faces of the nonmembers to them in their dreams. Indeed, to them, this was a normal thing to do; and this practice was formal for them.

Tuesday evenings were the days of the gamblers. The gamblers would assemble, set their seats in the most comfortable way for gambling, and proceed with their occupation. Some of these gamblers would spend almost all their week-long earnings on high stakes in anticipation of the mysterious lady-luck to bless them. Just a few would be favored by their *'god of fortune'*, while the rest would return home empty handed, their money, gone. Even as they lost all their money, their gambling addiction was always there to intoxicate them. They were so blinded in that they were always willing to come again to try, to spend the following week.

On Wednesdays, the liberal religious ones would take hold of their own rituals. These were the sects of the occult world. Here too, in this church building, they would gather to offer their sacrifices of praise; to the devils, to the arch-devils, and even to the mini-demons.

It was also on a Wednesday evening that Prince Kingsley witnessed the potential human sacrifice which made him both a villain and a hero in the sight of the people.

There were young school children who went to this church building on Thursday evenings to learn how to dance. Same day, at night, the college students would be here to spend the night away, dancing, drinking and making merry. Those who could not stand it would not stand it, would be better off staying in their college dormitories, studying or doing some other things.

On Fridays, the Muslim Members of the Society borrowed the church space to do their own thing. And on Saturdays those who believed in the ancient Decalogue: "Remember the Sabbath day and keep it holy" took the building and ritually sanctified it..

On the first day of the week, the true owners of the church building, the members of Universal Ecumenical Church, came in into their church building to serve their own God.

It was a neat arrangement. So neat that the idea was to accommodate all the other religious groups of the Kingdom, , who, without such an arrangement, would have accused the owners of the church building of "religious discrimination".

CHAPTER TWENTY-THREE (B)

In the early days of the invaders, discrimination was the pride of the conquerors. It was a pride voiced out in action. For example, the invaders felt so superior to the conquered natives, and this found constant expression, virtually in all places and even in all things. The Eminent Religious Maximuses were in the forefront in promoting their precious prejudice.

"Our God made it clear that night and day have nothing in common. What commonality has the house of the Lord and the house of the Babel? Therefore, we the civilized conquistadors and the conquered primitive, beast-like natives have absolutely nothing in common. Our God made it that way. And that is how it is going to remain forever" argued His Serene Highness (H.S.H), the Most Reverend Dr. B.B. Leotor, who embodied the exclusive religious station of the conquistadors. As the next thing to God in the land, whatever he said…even from his heart rich in prejudice…was the voice of the God of the conquistadors.

In essence, he propounded that the invaders from the North should have nothing to do with the primitive ways of the natives.

And in fact, he was one of the advocates who led the motion to herd the natives into the caged forests. Hence, as he caged them, he also kept them in constant watch, thus, to prevent them from a re-take-over of the conquered land.

"This is our land. Our God gave it to us" claimed the H.S.H before the peoples' Congress of Eminent Fellows. The members of this Ruling Party listened to his words with rapt attention.

His words made a lot of sense to them because their God gave them the land and they knew how they got the land. And they did not want their God to take it away from them and give it back to the natives. After all, didn't their God who said, 'Thou shalt not steal' also said, "Be strong and of good courage?" Therefore, they had to be strong and courageous enough to defend the land against any foe or friend, including their own God.

Later in the session, they knew the man nearer to God made a heck of a sense. And his endorsed motion was taken as an imperial security matter that called for no debates.

They knew they were in a precarious situation. With the land firmly in their hands, and the natives' anger at their heels, keeping the collective rage of the deprived natives under constant surveillance was the only way to secure the conquered land. As such, they did neither want to make any mistake…nor take any unwise chance.

At each of the entrance to the church hall was a double decked electric operated iron doors. These doors would open at the touch of the right electric square-shaped button.

Also, the doors could close at the touch of the right, square shaped "close" electric button. And both "open" and "close" buttons were located on the walls; that, just a foot from the doors.

CHAPTER TWENTY-FOUR

The leader of the Universal Ecumenical Church was a distinguished Priest. A man of saving talents whose church building was filled daily, with followers of different sects. He was so proudly convinced that he was a true servant of his own God. His heart was clear that he was a man of God.

He was devout and devoted. Overlooking his past, he looked forward to a better time in a global outreach, open-ended in the imperial world. Having seen both the dark and bright sides of life, he gave up the former to embrace the latter.

Among his flocks were those who kept their heads in the sand. The police men in the land, the guards of the Universal Ecumenical Church, and every member who knew the ways of the society, and the Supreme allegiance everyone in the Kingdom placed in the Supreme Duke.

The man who became a Priest was once a career criminal, a serial killer who organized and led a band of merciless bandits. He and his team terrorized the natives for a while before they extended their mission to those of their kind.

Once, they robbed an entourage of government officials. Five people dropped dead during the shoot-out. Two of his, a couple of foreign attaches, and an aid to a Governor.

The leader of these outlaws was captured. Together with thirteen armed members of his gang. They were all sentenced for life. These bandits were the notorious "missionaries of the deadly underworld". Sensationalized in newspapers, their reputation was known far and wide.

Two years later, the gang leader appealed his case. Upon the recommendation of the probate officer, there was another hearing, designed specifically for his case. A lighter sentence was given, and within six months he was paroled, and released.

Then, he gave up his soul unto the Lord. And he became a Christian. At twenty-five, he joined the Order of Priesthood, ministering to the lost world. When he became a man of God, one of the newspapers which depicted him as "the most evil element of our time" was ready to make amends. "The rebel angel has turned into an angel of mercy" wrote the editor of the newspaper in its headline.

Hardly had the Priest left when his wife picked up the phone to make a love pitch.

"Who's the devil?" a man's voice answered from the receiving end.

"If a tree falls in a forest and nobody saw it, does it make any noise?" she quipped back.

"Don't doodle with my time. I've told you I'm not interested" the man was angry. She had been making the moves to "connect with' him with less luck. It seemed to her, on those attempts, he didn't want to be involved in a married woman. But the woman was persistent; a possessive python who would not stop swallowing her prey until she had swallowed the prey from the prey's head to the prey's tail.

"Why don't you come over for spiritual counseling? It will do you good. We can pray for your law enterprise. The Lord will bless it, and your business will flourish" she argued. And her pitch played on his subconscious mind.

"But, what if this your spiritual counseling turned into an unhealthy bait-and-switch?" asked the man.

"I will not touch you. You know me" she re-assured him.

"Ma'am, are you sure?" the man retorted. He was not convinced yet. Suspicious, hesitant too.

"It may not happen; maybe a kiss. Why not give me a chance to explore possibilities? Are you afraid of romance?" she pitched.

"No, I'm not" he quipped back.

"Then, why delay. Common' over".

"Remember you're a Priest's wife. If you can't stay without a man, then buy a vibrator, stick it in your stuff and shake the organ till you feel good". He paused. Then, he continued "Second alternative, get a boyfriend to service you the way you want. Again, remember, there is a disease, I mean many. Venereal nosology shows there are more than ten different lethal venereal diseases spreading around".

"I've heard all that jazz. Common' over. Let's pray" she said, even as she gave him her verdict and hung up the phone.

CHAPTER TWENTY-FOUR (B)

A few minutes later, the man knocked at the door. And as soon as she opened the door, she held out her hands and seized him. She gave him a huge hug, followed by a whooping kiss on his two lips.

"Are you crazy? We've not even greeted?" the man protested.

"I've not kissed a man in three years" she quickly defended, her bad behavior, deflating his mild anger with an explanation for her lustful behavior.

"Common in" she held his hand, leading him into the bedroom. She kicked the door with her left heel. It closed. She did it, all in insouciance disposition.

"This place looks, smells good" the man began to notice.

"What kind of cologne have you on? It smells good" she did not only ask, she also gave her analysis, grinning in the process.

"It's just brut; it is inexpensive" answered the man.

"It smells good. I like it" she praised it.

"Thank you".

"I really mean it. I like the wearer, too" she honed in her point home.

"Thank you" he said again.

When the guest was comfortably seated, she brought out an old King James Version of the Holy Bible. She opened it. Turned to John Chapter three, verse sixteen and read. "For God so loved…" she stopped. 'With God all things are possible" she said. She closed the Bible, and she put it on a table.

"I need you every time" she said. She was now in total control of the situation. "Let's talk about Christ and race, O.K?"

"O.K. That's fine with me" the tensed man was by now more relaxed. She noticed that in him, too.

"You shouldn't be so formal with me" she said.

"I'm fine. I am quite relaxed" he replied. And as if to show her how relaxed he was, he took off his coat and gave it to her to hang. She did. Having done so, she sat down again.

"What do you know about our Lord Jesus Christ and the Libyan black man who did something for Christ when they were about to crucify him?" asked the wife of the Priest.

"When white men were about to crucify Jesus, it was the black man who came to the rescue" the man answered.

"Why don't I play the devil's advocate for the heck of it?" asked the woman.

"Please, ma'am, what do you mean?" asked the young man.

"What if I told you that the black man never carried the cross for the Son of the living God. What if I told you that it is all made up story" said the wife of the Priest.

"Do you doubt the word of God?" asked the young man.

That is not true. A black man did not help him" she disagreed.

"Why not re-study your scriptures? The crucifixion for example, where did Simon of Cyrene come from? From Europe?" argued the young man, a lawyer, A.J. John, J.D. (Doctor of Jurisprudence), her latest lover-to-be.

"I do not know where he came from. But" she paused. Abruptly, and she continued, "I don't think a black man should be smart enough to help our Lord and Savior to the cross".

"Madam", he changed from calling her ma'am to 'madam'. He looked serious, more professional. A lawyer ready to defend his case.

"Yes?" she responded with a question.

"What you are telling me is that if a black man should not be smart enough to help Christ, then the white men should be smart enough to kill him. Isn't that correct?" The lawyer nailed down his case. It stuck. He looked at her, watching for a counter-motion.

"I don't believe so much in biblical arguments. Why don't we talk about something else?" The defeated Priest's wife ventured to divert the topic. Her religious student was more knowledgeable than she. It showed.

"You invited me for Bible studies, right?"

"Yes, but I had something else in mind" she hinted a hidden agenda – An agenda best known to her.

"What is it?" The lawyer wanted to know.

"Let's talk about movies, relationships, love and…"

"And what?" the man shouted. Enraged, the woman had wasted his time, of course. "Movies? That's not why you invited me. That's no spiritual counseling. Is it?"

"Anything" she winked at him.

She was the wife of the Chief Priest, the most Serene Reverend. It had been their manner of things, hers and her husband's to invite guests over and entertain them with both perishable foods and with spiritual food. When the Priest was not home, his young wife would add some spice to the entertainment – By giving the guest, if a man, some physical entertainments.

Many of the young men in the parish knew the church leader and his wife well enough to understand them as a couple with generous hearts. The Priest had unbounded love for his wife, and unquestioning trust in her.

It was obvious that the couple were preparing their souls as well as the souls of those to whom they ministered to, for heaven. Because of their future hope, the Priest made it a parish paradigm to have an open-door policy. That, and so, to "who-so-ever would mayest come". The idea worked.

In matters of love, the Priest preached compassion. Every Sunday morning, he would exhort his church members to reach out to the needy. As the people used to say "action is a prophecy come true". When the thief repented, he changed.

On the other hand, the Priest's wife was a basket case in spiritual things, unbeknown to the husband. She pursued men like a demon-possessed nymphomaniac. And she was able to go to church service, every church day, using her husband's holy book to promote and conceal her secret lifestyle.

From the beginning, the Priest hardly knew nor understood the woman before he married her. She grew in a city. And she knew the ways of the city, especially the lifestyles of the city men.

One day, her former boyfriend invited her to a religious convention – as a new witness to the Lord. She followed. She liked excitement and loved to try out new things.

During the ministry, a man approached her and introduced himself. He wore a religious cloak. And he asked her whether she was married. She replied with a heart-warming, but to the Priest a re-assuring "no". It was a moment of bliss for an ex-thief who had lived in a voluntary celibacy for the last ten years.

"Today is my birthday. Today, I've met the woman of my dream. Boy, am I not lucky. Praise be to the Lord".

"Congrats Reverend" she said.

"Thank you" the thirty five years old Priest replied in his boyish baritone.

"Happy birthday to you, Rev".

"My joy will be complete with you as my help-meet".

CHAPTER TWENTY-FIVE

There was no doubt that the Holy Priest was truly in love. A Priest with a longing hope, the sight of the beautiful woman turned his spiritual table upside down. He had been a lonely man in a crowd of female converts; he was something similar to a thirsty sailor in a salty ocean of an abundant water. Still, like a jeweler in search of the special gem, he kept searching for the only one.

It was a love at the first sight. He asked her for her address, which she gladly gave. She introduced her boyfriend to the Priest as her brother. And the Priest bought the idea right away. Her lover was not ready for marriage yet. He preferred seeing the city girls, city women, city prostitutes for some time before making up his own mind. After all, he was a mere twenty four year old, barely graduated from a University of Technicalities, Xiayo, New Kingdom. He had the entire world ahead of him. So, why waste it with her?

Somehow, he viewed the Priest's presence as a stroke of good-luck. Because, for some-time, the young woman, who was ever-conscious of her biological clock, had pressed him to make some commitments. In each case, his response was:

"My dear, don't you think this is too early?" yes, it was 'too early' for him; but her biological clock was ticking 'too late' for her.

She wanted and needed a man just to get rid of her single lifestyle.

Two months later, the Priest and the woman were married. The Priest was so happy. He adored her the way a King would a virgin come into his life. She responded in kind by calling him "honey", "sweetie", "love" and "dear" most of the time.

She made him feel like the greatest man in the world. She went an extra mile to care for him, safe her secret desire for extra men. She was so discreet in her extra-marital affairs that she was able to cover her trails all along, every time. For example, oftentimes, her former lovers would come, one at a time, in the guise of her distant cousins. Each of these 'cousins' would spend some days with her and her trusting husband; each, enjoying the forbidden fruit in his absence, only to have the man of God tell his wife's lover 'please come again' when the lover was about to go home.

"Is your man impotent?" one of the 'cousins' who had visited the couple for more than ten times once asked her in the bed.

"No. He's perfectly all-right. But I'm a bad girl" she kissed him after calling herself 'a bad girl'. "I do whatever I wanna do. It's my body. I know how to play my cards". The woman made her points very clear to her lover.

For a while, the lover was wondering. He was aware of the fact that some married, impotent men would hire some able-bodied young men to render their sexual services to their wives. This was always done in discreet arrangement. In such a case, the impotent husband would consider it a special and invaluable favor. No doubt, the lover wondered.

One day, the Priest made an appointment to visit with a new neighbor, an actress, on the block. They had seen her walk past by the parish, to her studio, which was very close to the parish. On the first day the Priest saw the actress move into her new house, a thought to save her soul entered into his mind.

She had lived in the new neighborhood for three solid weeks before the Priest decided to make the move. Many nights on end, prior to his visit, the Priest and his wife would watch the actress on their "20 by 50" television screen. They were fascinated by the ways the unmarried young actress performed her job with reckless disregard for spiritual fulfillments.

Secretly, deep inside the Priest's wife were numerous unfilled vacuum…A longing to be like the actress – A desire to express herself cyber-punk 'X'-rated movies – To involve in sex-videogenic enterprises – And to pose for numerous cover-pages of pornographic magazines. She would dwell on these lofty pleasures, dreaming on for her lofty things, hours on end. That when her husband was far away, doing his own job of saving souls.

She was always discreet in her thoughts and in her actions. Never letting her guard down, lest her husband, the embodiment of Christian faith, know her true feelings – And her true self.

"The young actress needs salvation" he said to his wife. One evening, after watching the television show – the actress' television program.

"Yes, honey. We shall do everything we can to save her" she responded. Even as she responded to her loving husband, she remembered everything she did in the arms of her own lovers.

"Her soul is sliding into the everlasting fire" he said. And he painted those word-pictures in a way that made his wife to almost jump in terror, perhaps the terror of hell.

"Honey, I'm nervous. The Lord will help you. Please why not go to her tomorrow evening and talk with her. Please let us pray for her, sweetie. The Lord will save her, my dear" she said, visibly nervous. Whether she was jittery because of her own sins or high-strung due to her desire to save an actress from eternal doom, was an issue the Priest then did not know.

Her husband, ever-burning in an eternal hell of trust, knelt beside her. They prayed to their God for more than one hour that night before retiring to bed.

The Priest did not know that his wife had a hidden agenda that morning. As he was about to leave, he kissed her.

"I don't know how long I will impact the gospel unto her. Pray for me while I'm there. God willing, her soul will be saved" said the Priest.

"Yes, my dear. While you are there with her, my knees will be on the ground in prayers and supplications"" responded the wife of the Priest. Perhaps the actress' soul would be saved. But was the Priest aware of the unsaved status of his wife's soul? Future could tell.

"Please, pray fervently for her soul" the Priest said to his wife before he stepped out from the house.

"Honey, go ahead. May the Lord be with you" she had already leant how to speak in the language of her husband.

CHAPTER TWENTY-FIVE (B)

John was a lawyer, and her latest love on the line.

'I'm very nervous about this" the attorney said.

"Follow your heart" she advised him. Self-assured. That she was.

"If I do so, I will run away" he replied. That on the first day he visited her.

"Then follow mine" she was able to lead.

"Where will yours lead me to?" he asked. Not yet prepared for it.

"Hold on" she issued him an order. He held on. "Do you know why most black men go after our white women?" she asked.

"Piece of cake" the man knew the answer.

"Wait" she stopped him. "I will tell you. They say it is because of our kisses. Isn't that neat?" the love-sick woman asked.

"That's correct. White women can kiss a man everywhere: ear, mouth, neck, nose, chest, you name it. The black men love that" he added an advanced point to her answer.

"Well, what's up?" she asked. Twinkling her eyelids. She was ready to give him all those things.

"You've not answered my question as of yet. Where will your heart lead me to?" he asked her. Still reluctant.

The woman knew her answer tight away. In a way that sounded like a carefully rehearsed speech by an eloquent salesperson, she let go her tongue and the words came forth:

"To my bosom. To pleasure. To sweet things and longings…" Having said these, she positioned her mouth for him to take the lead.

By the way, this was on the first day; when the lawyer was hesitant and fearful to do the job that she wanted.

As time passed by, he became more involved. The days when he was hesitant and reluctant had passed. In passing, the romance became an overkill – A passion and a dance in the hell.

"Are you ready?" she asked him her favorite words. The last time her husband was gone.

"Ready".

"Ready to buy?"

"Okay, I'm sold" he said.

Then they began a drama in violent foreplay. The woman was on top of the man, instead of the man on top of her. She was doing the thing the way a man should have been doing it. Indeed, she was doing it faster than the rate a man would have been doing it. The lawyer was, as ever, amazed at the rapid speed of her buttocks' movements. And he could not hide his amazement, thrill and excitement.

"Legally speaking" he managed to say while she was still on top of him, "you are a magnificent woman".

"Enjoy me, darling" she replied, still pumping and pushing faster and harder on her speed pedal for greater acceleration.

When each stretch of speed had reached its peak, he would signal so. They would savor it, relax briefly, and start all over again. Again and again, he stretched out his hands and grabbed her. They kissed and kissed and kissed again. She held him as if to prevent him from ever running away from her. She squeezed him real good. He yielded. And they began anew to enjoy the forbidden fruit which was supposed to be an exclusive province of the Holy Priest.

CHAPTER TWENTY-SIX

Back in the actress's residence, the Priest pitched in for a special religious sale. He knew if he succeeded in redeeming her soul, she would not only be a great asset to the church's treasury, the Priest's reputation in the sight of his 'Holy God' would increase as well. And as his Priestly scripture said:

"Seek ye first the Kingdom of God, all these things shall be added unto you". And beside these, she would be a great connection to other stars in the money-rich pornographic industry.

And as far as the Priest was concerned, that particular piece of the scripture, even as he read it with his loving wife that morning, was a direct message from his God. He took those words so personal that he derived a new meaning from them.

When he was taking his morning shower, as it was his custom, a few words of the divine message were changed in his memory bank. And while he was stepping out from the bathtub, he opened his mouth to recite his new scriptural verse, "Seek Priest first the soul of actress, all her things shall be given unto you".

"Honey, what are you talking about?" His wife asked him. Her only question that morning.

"What did I say?" The embarrassed Priest said as he came to his senses.

"I don't know. You tell me" answered the pretty wife of the holy Priest. Quickly, he left the house. And he walked straight to the big house of the beautiful actress.

The actress and a guest were having a conversation, having a woman's talk – mostly talks about men, sex and stuff when the Priest, her neighbor, knocked at her door. He telephoned her earlier on to book for an appointment for a talk – a gospel talks.

Naturally, however, she was swept away by his trained voice over the telephone. But she was disappointed by his appearance when she opened her door to behold the man of God. In her own professional world fine impression was purely cosmetic. Anything devoid of this was promptly subject to disapprobation. Perhaps the Priest hardly knew. This and here, then and before, that mere artificial beauty was an overall picture of her cosmogony, its satellites, its potential rapture and indeed its eventual end.

"Please come in" she reluctantly invited her second guest of the day in.

"Oh, I've got to go" the other guest, a female, volunteered to give them, her hostess and her hostess's new guest, the Priest, their much-needed privacy.

"You don't have to leave" the honorable Reverend declared. Maybe her soul was needed too.

"Please don't go yet" her hostess pleaded.

"No. I've got to go. I have other fishes to fry" she quoted.

"If you insist. But I would…"

"Bye. See you later" she left.

"Miss, I will like to invite you to our Church on Sunday… It will be my honor to baptize you for the remission of your sins and the redemption of your soul. I know the Lord will richly bless you, give you power to overcome…" the Priest began to preach.

"Please I have a few questions. By the way, would you care for a cup of chocolate?"

"No. I've had my breakfast" he excused.

"Can I fix some for myself?" she requested.

"Sure. This is your kitchen, your house. Ride on" the man of God gave her his permission in her own house.

"I will be right back" she dashed into her kitchen. Soon after she was gone to an adjacent room, her kitchen, she returned with a steaming cup of hot chocolate. "This is my favorite drink. I don't like coffee. Uh, coffee is awful". She sat down directly in front of her guest in a pre-arranged loveseat in her parlor.

"Please, I have some question" she said again.

"Yes, go ahead. Ask me" the Priest replied.

"Please don't take my questions as being rude or an insult, because I wanna know".

"I don't think any question in the world can hurt my feeling" responded the man of God.

"I'm glad" she said. "Do you believe in God?"

"Yes, I do believe in God" he answered.

"Why in the world do you believe in God?" she asked.

"My dear, our God is rich in love, holiness and worthy to be praised" answered the Priest.

"Yes, I know. Why not give me some specific answers?" asked the beautiful actress.

"I will, my dear. There are three factors that made me to believe in God. First and foremost is God's intervention in my life. Second, is what is written in the scripture: for God is so loving: He sent his own son to die for me. Oh, what a wonderful God we have. And last, but not the least, nature or natural: Both living and non-living things which are evident results that a higher force is for sure in control of this world.

Spiritually speaking though, it's not what one believes but what one practices that scores the point".

"That's fine" the actress commended.

"Thank you, my dear" said the man of God.

"Go ahead" the actress smiled and responded.

"Would you please describe God for me?" asked the man of God.

"You are the expert. Please tell me. I am now your student. I am always ready to learn from a good teacher" said the actress.

"According to the scriptures, 'God is a very Powerful Spirit and those who worship Him must worship Him in Spirit and in truth'. The same scriptures told us that 'God created man in His own image'. Now, should I go even further, nature and even some distant tribes testify that God is One. Moreover, in a certain African tribe, the name "God" is pronounced "Chineke". This "Chineke" means 'one who creates; and his creative power, as such is very continuous.

Naturally though, we have never seen God, our only point of descriptive reference is this: Man is made in the image of God…"

"Why man, why not include woman?" the actress interrupted the man of God.

"God is man…"

"I don't like that…" she was a feminist.

"Please I shall explain this to you. The word 'man' is generic"

"That's better. I can live with that".

"Thanks be to God. God is spirit, and that for sure, the Supreme Creator, always in action…"

"Sir, I have another question. Do you believe in abortion? I mean keeping it safe and legal?" asked the actress.

"God forbid. I will not ever think of marrying a woman who will ever dream of murdering my baby in her holy womb" the Priest answered.

"You don't know what you are talking about. Women are in control of their wombs. Men have no power over them" said the actress.

"That's nonsense. How can my wife decide to kill a kid that doesn't belong to her alone?" replied the Priest with a question.

"It is her body. The fact that a man deposited his male-seed in her womb does not mean that she is his incubator for babies. Does it?" asked the actress.

"Hello, her body is the temple of the Holy God. Anyone who dares to defile it is subject to everlasting damnation in the terrible hell of fire. This is no joke, my dear".

"Wait a minute. If your holy God is so cruel as to push every woman that removed unwanted pregnancy, then, such a God cannot be my God. Three men raped me when I was in secondary school. My father did not advise me to allow the seeds of the rapists to grow and turn me into an unwed mother of many bastards. He paid the doctors who saved me from such unmerited shame…"

"He should not have done that. Who knows if the murdered babies could have become the Great Saviors of our world…" said the Holy Priest.

"So, you think my father sinned against your God?"

"Unfortunately, he did. His sins were sins against the Holy Ghost. Neither God the Father, nor Christ, His Son, nor the Holy Ghost would ever forgive such unpardonable sins" answered the man of God.

"No, you are wrong. I think, you are twisting the word of God" said the actress.

"No, I do not. Rather, what you and your father did to the innocent babies were unpardonable crimes"

"Really?" asked the actress.

"Yes, really" answered the Holy Priest.

"I see. I see. Yeah, I can't help but profess, here and now that there are many demons hiding in the church as men of God" said the actress out of anger.

"You are damn right about that" agreed the Priest. "But, what can we do to eliminate them?" he asked. Perhaps she thought he would defend the demons, including those demons that tell women to commit abortion. But she was wrong.

"Hm, impossible" she said taken unaware.

"Nothing is impossible under the sun" responded the Priest.

"I still believe so. If not, well, let me put it this way; he who is eating with the devil from the same plate or bowl must use a long fork…"

"You mean we must only be careful and let the sleeping dog lie?" the Priest charged in a challenging question.

"Exactly".

"You are insane" the Holy Priest put it to her.

"Not exactly, it is a word of wisdom, the wisdom that demands some solutions" she disagreed.

"We are going to pray about it" the Priest gave a ready solution.

"That's fine, but didn't the church people 'prayer without work is in vain?'" she asked.

"Yes, all in vain that prays without work" he agreed, that in answering.

CHAPTER TWENTY-SIX (B)

While the Holy Priest was busy preaching, arguing, prodding, inducing, challenging and rebuking his potential convert, his own wife was busy too doing her own thing. Her nipples were erect, like a set of thing that belonged to the man; gorged out and vibrating at every push; their temperature was high, exceeding the mammary boiling point.

The Priest looked at the actress. He could look at other people, except for his own wife, and read their minds like a holy book.

"I have an offer which you cannot refuse" said the Holy Priest.

"What is it?" the actress asked him.

"Here". He gave her two books, a Holy Bible and another book, "How to become a great Christian". He was a good salesman, marketing not only himself, his ideas, his own book as well.

"Good books?" she asked, eager to open and read.

"This is a bridge between all".

"What all?" she wanted to know

"All human races" he supplied the answer.

"Uh huh. How?" she needed an answer.

"Our human races are separated by shapes. Sins of intolerance. Sin of not seeing that our separate shapes are blessings, not a curse. Sin of being blinded from appreciating square shape, triangular shape, round shape or any other shape of human head as good and sound. Sin…"

"Enough" she shouted. "Enough of your sermon".

"I am chosen to preach the gospel. To condemn evil and not to condone it, to expose sin not to ever espouse it, to preach the food of life on the mountain top…"

"I said, shut up! Don't preach to me. You should go to the leaders and tell them all these sermonic nonsense" she redirected the Holy Priest to the right people who truly deserved to hear the gospel of truth.

"Yes, my message is also meant for them…" the Priest did not disagree.

"Then, why not go to them. Why not tell them to stop bribery and corruption. To stop wars and starvation. To stop suffering and increase…"

"Hallelujah" the Priest shouted in the middle of her speech.

"What?" she asked him. She wanted to know why he interrupted her, and what the word 'hallelujah' meant.

"The Lord has chosen you to preach the good news too. Hallelujah, you are going to make a difference…" he said.

"Hold it there. You want me to be like you? Doing this kind of thing? No way. You are not doing anybody's business. It's all yours" she said.

"I am helping you. You should understand that. My mission is to save you from eternal damnation".

"But you get paid for your job. Don't you?" the actress reasoned with a question.

"Yes…"

"And you want me to leave mine and come and work for you without pay?' she proceeded to ask.

"All I'm asking you to do is to surrender your life to the Lord" answered the Holy Priest.

"Why?" asked the actress.

"Because the Lord saves. And the Lord desires to save your soul".

"In what Bank?" asked the curious, porn-actress.

"I am not talking…"

"Tell me the name of the bank, his account number, I will go there right now and see how much he has in his bank account".

"You don't understand" said the man of God.

"What do you mean?" asked the actress.

The actress was a lady who was brought up with the ideas that, "Money makes a man" and "A womanhood could only be attained when a girl ate the forbidden fruit".

It was because of these ideas that made her to ask him how much "The Lord" had in his bank account information. Besides, she was impressed by his charm and eloquence, despite his unimpressive appearance. She desired him. But she was afraid too. She held her guard, refraining from showing off, lest the man of God rebuke or put a curse on her.

She would forever treasure her first true love – The first mature man to ever kiss her from toe to head. She remembered how, after kissing her, asked her to put her tongue into his ear. And she did. It was her greatest moment.

She felt transported to the moon when the man gave her the most hilarious romance she had ever had.

"I love it; I love it" she shouted hilariously.

"When did you get all these ideas?" she asked him, instead of 'where', her longing, ever-engaged eyes fixed on him.

"Wait, there is more on board" he answered.

"Wow, you're a naughty boy" she replied.

"I'll make you a bad girl" he added.

"God, make my day" she said, calling her lover her 'God'.

But this Priest was a different man. He viewed things differently. His hope was not in love canal. His dream was not made up of carnal love. And his desire was to redeem her soul. That, from eternal damnation.

"Christ does not put his money in the bank; he treasured them in heaven…"

"Wow" she exclaimed and smiled.

The evangelist smiled too.

"I know your life is worldly…"

"There you go again. Do you and I not live in the same world? How can we pretend that this is no longer the world we live in?" she questioned.

"That's why I said you just do not understand the mysteries of the future hope to be revealed" answered the Priest.

"You got me. But tell me mister…"

"I am a minister of the gospel. You should address me as "Reverend". The Priest corrected her.

"I'm sorry".

"Your sin is forgiven" said the man of God.

"Hm, your way of talking amuses me, though. The other day you promised me a big house, to live in when I die, if I should follow you" said the porn star.

"That's correct. Repent and be baptized, you shall be saved. And the eternal mansions in heaven shall be yours".

"Will they be bigger than the one you live in by the ocean-side?" she asked the Priest.

"The mind cannot imagine and the eyes have never seen what the Lord has in store for those who hearken to his laws" answered the Holy Priest.

"There you go again talking in figurative terms, in the language of your unrevealed mysteries" she put in a light-hearted jest. Wide-eyed. Still.

"The Lord knoweth those who are his. For the sheep understandeth the voice of their shepherd and the shepherd heareth their voices" responded the Priest.

"Okay oh" she gave in, unable to argue.

"That's correct" he affirmed.

"Let us get down to business. I am a business woman. I do not work for free. Tell me: How much will that Lord of yours pay me, if I worked for him? Remember, I am an actress. I am comfortably fine with where I am and…"

"Unless a man will leave all his earthly belongings, yeah, even his mother and father and follow me, he is not worthy of me" the Priest quoted.

"That is outrageous" responded the female porn-star.

"Yeah, it is easy for a camel to go through the eye of a needle than a rich man to enter into the Kingdom of God" said the Holy Priest.

"I am beginning to see the light. You are a rich man. Aren't you?" she asked.

"Not in worldly sense".

"No oh Reverend. Common now. You have a mansion by the ocean-side plus one you and your family live in at the parish. You have a yacht, a stretch of limousine and a couple of Mercedes. Are you going to leave them? If so, to whom?"

"This is not what we are talking about, my dear" the Priest disagreed with the porn-star.

"Reverend, I hate hypocrisy. I do not like double-tongue. You said unless a man leaves all his properties and his parents, yet you are now telling me 'this is not what we are talking about'. What the hell are we talking about?' she shouted at him.

"Please let us re-schedule this discussion. I will like to go home and re-study the scriptures to be able to provide you with the answer" the Priest said.

"Wait" she grabbed his hand. "By the way, Reverend, don't you find me attractive?" the single actress, having overcome her fear, suddenly found herself asking the married Priest. She looked lovingly in his face, longing for a positive answer.

"Yes, the Lord knows I do. But your soul is more important than transient pleasure of the flesh" the soul-minded man of God replied.

Quickly, she let go his holy hand. Enraged. She did no longer want him to stay.

"Bye. Don't ever come here again unless you've studied your holy scripture well enough to give me un-hypocritical answers to my questions. You got that?" the enraged actress barked. Disappointed, she was, in her sexual overture.

"I shall do my best" the Priest stood. He had to leave.

Otherwise, she could make up something and accuse him of sexual harassment – which would have, doubtless, ruined his religious career, forever.

"Your best is not enough" she countered.

"Please" he begged.

"Un-hypocritical answers. Nothing more, nothing less. You get that?" she shouted at her guest again who was by this time on his feet making his way to the door.

"Yes, my dear. God willing, I shall" answered the man of God.

CHAPTER TWENTY-SEVEN

"There was a lunatic in the cellar" when the Priest got home. This was a way the people of the New Kingdom used to say whenever an unpleasant surprise awaited someone right in his own bed.

When the holy man left his house to preach to the actress, his wife hastily phoned her lover to come to the rescue. She thought he would stay at least eight hours, as he was wont of doing in a similar evangelism; this time, however, it was a different story. He returned earlier than usual.

She married him because she needed a husband. And beside this, he was a rich man. She knew that love, as ever, was the essence of a lasting marriage. Somehow, along their love-path, she came to a vantage enlightenment; an idea that true love, in itself, was distinct from any kind of lustful, physical attraction. This was her spiritual baptism as preached and practiced by her holy husband.

The woman knew herself so well as to seal all her dirty skeletons away from the cupboards, where her husband kept all their clean cups. It was this stray in spiritual consciousness that turned her into straying into the arms of other men.

When the lover arrived, they went straight into the bed, kissing and doing the thing.

"He's gone" she said.

"Great". He replied. "When the cat is gone…?"

"The mice play" she answered; kissing him passionately. They kissed longer and even longer. He swept her from two legs; carrying her gently, delicately and kissing her gingerly even unto her husband's bed. In there, they sat and romanced for a while.

The bedroom was located on the second-floor of the parish mansion. Adjacent to the bed was a grand-dad alarm clock. And a couple of steps away from it, was a bed, hide-away couch.

"Let's use coach" she suggested. She knew some fluids from their romance could reveal her secret affair. She wanted to prevent it. The man knew. He agreed, and he obliged. This was not the first time they had done it in the hide-away bed. Unlike the first time, they did it, fighting like two angry dogs, the following ones and including this last one, they did not argue again. Their first encounter broke the magic spell of argument, after which, it was all bliss.

"That's true". He said. He should have said "O.K" But he read her mind. He placed her feet carefully on the floor, like an ornithologist placing a delicate robin's egg in its nest.

He stood up. Looked around, then he stole away from the bed; closer to the couch he stepped; carefully he moved like a professional thief in the middle of the night.

Carefully, he pulled out the hide-away bed from the couch. She helped him set the bed in a proper way. Hardly had they began a sixth round when the entrance door opened.

"He's back" she said. When she said it, the man on top of her was terrified.

"Damn; I'm done. What shall I do?" said the love-thief.

"Calm down" the woman said. She was the manager of the whole situation.

"Sure. I am calming down" said the male-concubine.

"You must hide" said the wife of the Holy Priest.

"Where?" asked the male-concubine. By this time the Priest was very close to the innermost door.

With a thrust by his head, the lover disappeared through the asbestos ceiling roof. He held tight unto the other side of the ceiling fan.

While the Priest was trying to open the bedroom door, his wife folded the hide-away bed, hid it in its place and concealed the space left, or the space created by her lover who was by now temporarily safe in the ceiling.

The returning Priest, though faithful to his wife, was provoked to passion; doubtless, the actress who he wanted to save, used her feminine charm to ignite his passion for his wife.

It was an instant chemistry, a redox-reaction to lose himself unto his wife, and to gain her love into his arms. She tried, all in vain, to talk him into going away that late afternoon from the house to do something else. His masculine chemistry was at its peak reaction. The optimum point where a man would not mind the risk, provided the price would help him satisfy his urge. Afterall, this woman was his own wife. He did not want to misbehave with another woman.

So, he decided, since this one was his own woman, to enjoy her bosom right away…even without hesitation.

"I'm not ready now, darling" she pleaded.

"Oh, honey, give it to me, right now. My dear, you don't have to be ready to get into this unique divine show" said the man of God. He showered her with one rainy dose of kisses after another. Each rainy dose was heavy.

"Why not go away for at least ten minutes so I can make this as romantic as possible?" she tried to dissuade him. But the fire in him did not quench.

"No dear, you're more romantic than Adam's Eve of Eden". The Priest brushed away his wife's excuse; pushing and mounting a fierce penetration.

"Please, take it easy" she protested.

"Oh no my love. My love for you burns faster than the fire in hell. To stop is no option" said the man of God.

She could no longer resist. He had already made the penetration, overcame her resistance in the process. As he enjoyed it, her soul went forth to the delicate secret above the ceiling.

They did the thing for about one hour, still the man was in desperate need for more.

"Honey" she called, devising another reasoning tactic "I'm tired now; let's take a walk and have some fresh air".

The man's hand reached out and pulled a string that turned on the ceiling fan.

"Here we go; your fresh air" the Priest replied. He had solved her "air" problem without even taking a walk. He smiled as the fresh, sweet air breezed down from the ceiling fan. The fan on the ceiling rotated faster and faster, showering its breeze on the man and his wife.

All the while, the lover in the ceiling was holding tight to the iron pole connecting the fan to the roof. As the fan rotated, the iron-pole vibrated and he felt a sensation of shock. He did not want to die. As he tried to walk away from the danger, the square-shaped asbestos ceilings, gave way, one after another.

"Oh-h-h." The man fell on top of the bed. "God brought me here". The lover managed to say.

"Honey, let's run away" the Priest's wife said. But the man stood his ground, startled though he was.

"Who are you?" The Priest asked.

"Sir. God brought me here" the lover managed to say again.

The Priest's wife, seeing her last trick foiled, felt ashamed of herself. Nevertheless, she was the manageress of her situation.

"Who are you?" she asked, less assertive than in her usual voice. Still in bed; this time and somehow trying to cover her nakedness.

The man, the Priest, by this time was way away from the bed. Firmly stood on his feet, obviously ready to fight this intruder who claimed that "God brought me here". He looked at his wife and her lover; both naked, and both now in the bed.

"Honey, what is happening here?" The Priest questioned. Her shame and sense of guilt overwhelmed her.

"Honey, I' am sorry" she pleaded.

"I don't understand" said the man of God. Indeed, her husband disagreed.

"I said, God brought me here. Now let me go" said the naked intruder. And he made an attempt to walk out from the bed.

"Wait a minute. Who are you?" the Priest asked him.

"That question is not necessary. Your God brought me here. Now, get me out of here" demanded the naked intruder.

By this time, the lover stood in front of his lover's husband.

"Who are you?" the Priest asked, still again.

"Irrelevant. I wanna leave, now" replied the intruder. That's right.

"Irrelevant" that's what the lover said. It was 'relevant' for him to milk from the Priest's cow, but irrelevant for the Priest to know who he was. The lawyer knew the language of law very well. He thought he knew the law more than the Priest of God. "Irrelevant", that's fine. It was "irrelevant" to question him even though God brought him there.

Perhaps the lawyer thought he would be able to twist the truth again, as he had done many times in the peoples' court – especially when he was defending some of his criminal clients; twist the truth as usual to his legal advantage and twist the truth with the man of God. But the man of God was ready for him and for his lover as well.

Lawyers in the New Kingdom were so trained that they were the "Spotless Hearts of the Society". And, whatever they did were bound to be crime-free. And Attorney John knew a colleague who advertised in a telephone directory. "Do anything. Call me. I can defend you". You see, with the law behind a lawyer's crime, "anything" there was equal to "Spotless".

"Please let him go" the woman in the bed pleaded.

"I am not holding him. Am I?" her husband questioningly disagreed with her.

"John, don't come here again. I don't want trouble in my marriage" the woman shifted the blame and placed it on her lover alone. The Priest got the idea. His wife was having affairs.

"This is nonsense. Absolute nonsense. Honey, who is this guy? What is going on here?" He shifted from addressing his wife to her lover. "Friend, whoever you are, you are not leaving this place until I know how God brought you here". The Priest stepped out from his bedroom, banged the door closed. He locked it with his own key.

"Honey, open the door". His wife banged the door, pleading from inside.

The Priest anticipated that his wife might have the spare key, with no delay, he took an instant precaution. He bolted the door from his own side, quite secure.

CHAPTER TWENTY-EIGHT

The woman was stripped of all her religious gratuities, merited and unmerited ones. The most devastating blow came upon her when another lawyer, this time a woman, paid her a visit in a makeshift home. She was a divorce lawyer, and was a real professional in her own field.

Already, the separated wife of the Priest became a marked woman to those with whom she was sharing the new temporary place of abode.

"Are you the wife of the Priest?" the professionally dressed young lady asked her.

"Yes, unfortunately".

"Are you doing o.k.?" The female lawyer asked her.

"Here I sit broken hearted. I came to shit and only farted. It's tough. I won't tell you a lie. Life goes on" answered the would-be ex-wife of the Holy Priest.

"Don't give up hope" the lawyer consoled her.

"I'm hanging in there" the potential ex-wife accepted her psychological consolation.

"All things will be fine" the lawyer added, preparing her for the real blow.

"I hope it will" the woman who said she was 'hanging in there' is now hoping.

"It was my body, not my mind that put me into this pit".

"Ma'am, your body and your mind are the same. Maybe it was your desire" said the lawyer.

"I guess so" responded the would-be ex-wife of the Holy Priest.

"Oh, lest I forget, this is for you" the lawyer took out an enveloped piece of letter from her handbag. "I hope you would not take it too hard. It is from your husband, a notification for divorce, that's what it is. I am his attorney".

"Oh, my God, how can I survive?" the woman jumped on her feet; quite hysterical.

"Ma'am, this is not the end of life" answered the attorney.

"It is for me" she threw back at the divorce lawyer.

The lawyer did not want to wait to observe all her reactions. After all, she had accomplished a segment of her mission – to make sure the Priest's wife got the notice.

Her lover who put her in trouble became a man at large. He left the New Kingdom without leaving a trace.

Here was a woman whose ruling passion was to secretly and forever cheat on her husband, enjoy the unspiritual thing. Caught in her own net, she was now on a thorny race against time. It was a race against a hostile time.

The odds were heavy, set and complete, all in a total and mortal combat against her. Had she known, but the time was too late. She married a man who believed not only in her purity before marriage, but also in fidelity while in the same marriage. Somehow, she just could not cope.

She knew a different world before she was married into the religious world. Being already set in her own old world, it would have been tough to live in the new one without a good mask to bear it through.

Her husband could no longer have her; the church disfellowshipped her; and her lover abandoned her. All her sense of connection, lost in the fine prints. In the end, all that mattered were her thoughts on how she would be able to survive, put a roof over her head, and get on with her new life. Tough indeed, the new life her love-life created, made her a very different woman.

"How can I survive? Everything I worked for is gone" the ex-Priest wife complained to an employee at "Organization for Abused Women". She was ready to talk with the employee who was ready to hear. That was the employee's job. To listen to the 'abused women' talk about their problems; take notes of her bitter complaints and to make some recommendations.

There were so many of this type of "Organization" in the New Kingdom.

The ex-Governor's lover formed this very chapter soon after she got out of a three-year term imprisonment on account of child molestation. She was giving it all her energy, the type of energy level she was expending on digging for many men's gold from their pockets.

Kingsley was a part time worker in one of the newly established offices of the organization. He was putting in a few hours for pay, daily, in helping out the abused women. The ex-Governor's love came to like him because of his charm and work performance. These days however, she was very careful with men.

She did not want to do anything that would make her to ever see again the gate of the penitentiary. She had enough of it. And those enough times behind bars were more than enough for her.

Witnessing on daily basis, the real physical abuse among inmates was very common. Watching some nerve-racking physical fights between some crime-hardened prisoners was more than a torture for her. After some of those fights, one or two people would be buried unceremoniously as a result of each of the fights. And the sight of the dead, after each fight, would not even deter the other potential fighters, from fighting. Rather, it became an inducement to stage a more fierce fight; it became a new perspective between every two fighters – kill her before she killed you.

There were so many millions of people in the world in those days, as in nowadays, yet, so many so lonely. And her days in the penitentiary offered her a unique opportunity to enjoy a first-class experience in loneliness, though in the midst of other criminals.

"I love money, but not so new" she said as she tried to separate her new currency bills which were sticking together.

"I'm praying that I'm not pregnant" said the newest abused woman being counseled in her office. She had made her payment twice the usual fee because her case was urgent.

"Why?" the Executive Director, the ex-convict asked her

"My dear boyfriend is not supportive" said she. The Director sat up on her seat. Speechless for a while.

"Life is tough until you begin to make good use of it. You can profit from my experience".

"I've heard about it. You've been doing a wonderful job" said the young lady who was afraid of getting pregnant.

"Thank you".

"Why not write a book about it?" the young lady suggested to her executive counselor to whom she paid the 'not so new' currency bills. "I'm sure it will sell".

"Good idea. But I don't know any literary rep…"

"It's easy".

"Really?"

"Yeah, of course. I've got some leads. I can bring you some names when I come back tomorrow; will that be alright?".

"That will be marvelous".

"It's a deal. I will like to read your book" the abused client got excited for her.

"Sure, yeah; I've got another idea".

"What is it?"

"Ghost writers. I'm a very busy person, you know. A ghost writer can do a good job as well. What do ya think?"

"There are many of them around. They are professionals, too. The trouble is, you split the royalties with them".

"I don't care. Get me their names".

CHAPTER TWENTY-NINE

The actress developed an instant and a keen interest in the Universal Ecumenical Church soon after the Priest got a divorce. It was an uncontested legal case because matrimonial infidelity was a shallow ground for an alibi. She, the adulteress, was a no show at the court and the verdict was rendered against her.

"I'm going home to stay at home, otherwise my wife 'be kicking off my ass', you know what I mean?" the victorious Priest said to some news reporters who wanted to know how he felt after the verdict. The case was televised. The actress, having known what was happening between the Priest and his adulterous wife, saw to it.

The Priest's wife, now ex, was smart enough to save herself the paramount humiliation. She has been disgraced enough already.

"Tell us Reverend, if you would not mind, what you've learnt from this experience" a reporter pointedly asked the Holy Priest. After asking the question, many reporters closed in their microphones to the Priest's mouth for a response.

"Never bet on horses, weather or women" the Priest replied. Most of the reporters including the female ones, laughed at the Priest's remarkable response. If there were any consolation to the Priest for his failed marriage, it would be the prime affection which the actress was ready to provide him.

The actress was now a chorus girl before she made it big in her acting career. Once an auditioning agent, after watching her cast in for an acting role, told her "break a leg".

In the acting career, that in itself was a good omen. Indeed, the following events were histories of success. She got it made with the help of the same fore-sighted agent who made himself her exclusive agent. Making such box office movies as "Kqakum Love", "Ajudu on the Moon" and "The Day Sun Died" solidly established her career as a worthy actress. Huge sums of money rolled in as fast as her popularity soared throughout the New Kingdom and beyond. Yet, she was single. Yet, many men avoided to bless her with her supreme desire – a committed man in her life.

It was said in the New Kingdom, men were easily intimidated by women who were much richer than they were. Such was indeed a truth – the truth that brought the men's pseudo-machorisms to the limelight. Thus depriving otherwise good women the true love of marriage and children gotten in wedlock, simply because they happened to be so rich. Such were the prices most of the rich women in the land were paying because they were favored by the gods of financial abundance.

In the beginning, her lust for the Priest was, in the matters of spiritual enlightenment, a case of weir-do. But this time however, the woman who claimed the soul of the Priest's trust, had voluntarily taken herself out of the hub. She'd learnt from acting experience, that one of the ways to win friendship, advance one's career and become a partner in an enterprise, was to be a team player.

The woman's misadventure was, to the actress, an opportunity for her to get into the man's life. The time she begged to be accepted, in a snap, vanished away. This time, the man needed what she had been willing to offer. So she would go into him in style, with class, and by all the charms her profession had to offer. No turning back, because the man would no longer resist her.

"Can I buy you another black biretta? I know you can buy it. I don't mean to insult you" the actress asked the Priest's permission to buy him a religious cap. The one he wore every Sunday morning was not new. It was not very old either. It was just fine if kept clean enough for the purpose.

"Please do whatever you want. I won't be offended. Never" the Priest gave her his whole-hearted permission.

"Can I buy you a purple or a red instead? I don't like black color very much" the actress engaged him closer in the conversation.

"I'm not yet a Bishop. Purple is for a Bishop, red for a Cardinal. Black will be just fine. You don't have to buy me any, if you don't want to".

"No. I want to buy you some, as many as you want. They look good on you, really" she gave up her stand, fearing lest she lose him.

CHAPTER TWENTY-NINE (B).

There was no doubt that Madam Cecilia Ashahuru was the devil in the Church. Everyone knew her as a strong-willed woman. She was the black dragon, too righteous for a man to reproof.

From the day she became a convert, after thirty years of intercourse with the art of witchcraft, she made it crystal clear that she came in to take control of the parallel sect. She was baptized quite alright; and her baptism was a day of mixed feeling, joy and merriment. Hardly had she become a full-fledged member than she adopted her own version of practical Christianity. To force it down the throats of others – whether they agreed to or not.

The baptism took place three months after the Priest got the uncontested divorce. By this time, he was seeing the young actress in a romantic way. Somehow, the Priest did not share in the joy of his flocks. As they rejoiced for the redemption of the old witch, he feared for the worst thing the witch-lady might bring upon his dominion. He was fearful for his own life, his career, fearful for the safety of members of the church, and not least for the soul of the new convert whose fearful reputation was very controversial in the land.

It was the beginning of realization of the Priest's worst fear. The Priest was not happy, neither were the members of his church committees after the meeting was over.

It all happened. During one of the monthly meetings of the Committee of Elders, the latest converts, Madam Cecilia Ashahuru, showed up. Uninvited. These Elders were not only all men, they were also the pillars of the Ecumenical Church.

When she came, she came up with an idea on how to run the church. She was a business woman, a very rich one so,

She came up with a plan to set up an 'advisory office for women'. This, she said, would help the female members play more active roles in the ministry. She implied that an office would be necessary. She imposed that the office must be constructed in the parish in a way that it would be facing the office of the Priest.

The ten Elders of the church plus the Priest were terrified by her commanding eloquence. And they all yielded to her verbal pressure out of fear.

During the so-called discussion meeting, however, a committee member suggested to put the idea on hold because of financial constraints. Thereupon, she made a pledge to finance, furnish, and staff the entire program.

Toward the end of the meeting, she pledged to be the "Director of Advisory Office for Women". As far as Madam Cecilia was concerned, the church had been too busy having fun. It was time to put hands on the dirty ground and get down to the real business. Maybe she was right about the church. Just, maybe so.

Madam Cecilia had the money to finance her pledge. A resident of 66% Millionaire Highway, an exclusive area where some of the richest men in the New Kingdom lived. A few women owned palaces and mansions in this very exclusive area. Madam Cecilia, as she was fondly called, was one of them.

It was the age of dual events. Surely, preachers would preach, but their actions would preach otherwise. Those who were wise and upright among them sought other occupations in-spite-of the luxuries their first love held in store for them.

Politicians would promise one thing and deliver another; they provided in sheer mockery, no excuses for any of their actions. Brutalities were known everywhere, all over the land. The police officers were able to gain promotions, only by the wings of corruption. In homes men would beat their wives, and the beaks and talons of the law would quickly be on the side of the law-breakers; older kids would violate the younger ones with impunity, and on and on the crimes soared. And in some cases, some women would shoot their husbands on charges of self-defense or for anything that came into their twisted minds. And as quickly as some money exchanged hands, the open crimes morphed into acts of righteousness.

Schools were not even safe. From grade schools to universities, everyone had a right to bear arms and to use same in self-defense. Kindergarten kids were allowed to hold toy guns till they were old enough to bear the real ones.

A kindergartener had a right to sue a teacher for violating his rights of privacy. For example, if the kid were a boy and the teacher, a woman, the tension would be even higher. The teacher would not change a soiled kid's diaper without the kid's due permission. And the same would be sued for damages and professional negligence, if she happened to fail to serve the very moment the child pointed an attention to his special need.

As kids, they were the new owners of the land. And as the owners of the land, they were supremely unique in so many ways. Among them were people who found it extremely difficult to smile. Smile-less-ness was the norm and a thing that the people prided themselves in. It was treasured as a fiber of their sound civilization.

There were, however, immigrants to the land, who felt ill-at-ease at this unpalatable fiber of civilization. These were immigrants whose culture laid overwhelming emphasis on such a social grace as smile-full-ness in the land of their birth. A treasure that should not be parted away. This difference in outlook was the culture gap. And a very big one so.

This culture gap, in passing, brought many a set of misunderstanding, misinterpretation, quarrel and marginalization between the newcomers and the old dwellers. Its other effects were stiff as well. Anger, hatred and distrust were there. These were outgrowths of culture gap, culture shock and culture slap. The gap was wide. An outlook with variable changes internalized in people of variable cultural backgrounds, domains, attitudes and viewpoints. Culture fights were intense and so many.

There were some immigrants who found it difficult to give up their old ways in favor of those obtainable from their new home. Cultural preservation rather than cultural surrendering was emphasized, so often, by each of the ethnic entities. Every culture wanted to be well known.

The stronger cultures stood the tests of the days. If powerful enough, survived, thrived and subdued the weaker ones. For example, Chiboha-language perished, was buried and resurrected. The old language was once again subdued and replaced with a new one brought in by the conquistadors. Today, it's only a fraction of the old language that survived.

It was also the age of dual deeds. Foreign ideas were sources of irritation. Red-baiting was abundant. And medical McCarthysm scared the medical doctors away from better medical practices.

An era a few medical doctors invented suicide machines, to kill their patients instead of finding cures for their terminal diseases, rose and became the norm. The same medical McCarthyysm was an era when good physicians feared to practice medicine and a period practical medicine stroke terror in the hearts of the patients.

CHAPTER TWENTY-NINE (C)

It was a period of multiple medical malpractices and a season of intense medical litigation. A cold winter of abortions and the sunny summer of rapes.

Yes, it was the sun-lights of abortions after the summer-nights of open rapes. A windfall of seduction. And a season everyone was free to gratify his or her indulgence. And a season of the horrible disease known as aids.

An age devoted professionals went to their lucrative jobs with their thoughts somewhere else. For many a hard time. And for a few, an easy time.

A time when a "Billy Token" would be so proud-less of his shattered heritage and so willing to token out himself, his family and even his self-worth. A moment a conquered fellow would be proud whenever he was accepted by those who conquered him.

It was an age the poor folks were mocked to resentment. And a time when time itself never seemed to fly. It was a time when things never seemed would change.

It was the age certified virgins would prefer to have the oral sex – A deadly combination of sinful dreams and selfish righteousness. And a mortal struggle between spiritual life and physical lust.

It was the period of less regard for marriage; and a period of unmarried would advertise for the same.

Here was the age patriotism was the main identifying quality of nationalism. It was also the decade the gods deadened their senses from dictating the mortifying follies of men.

There they were. It was when living faith grew old. A time faith was built purely on self and detached from every non-self.

In good measure, a state in human view when anything posing as a deity was closely defined as a state of mind. Besides, it was the age men were willing to deceive themselves. People were known by the occupations they held. Each occupation in itself was the only means to his worth. It was the age of greed, of great greed and even of sound greed.

It was indeed the passionate moment of eminent greed – A season of identity crises of the holiest type. A moment in time man showed a reckless disregard for the power on high.

It was a time man showed his supreme confidence, and a time he reflected an abysmal lack of it. It was only a period of spiritual over-confidence, a period of lack there-of as well.

This was the interrupted continuum of spiritual indulgence. It was a time man gave reason not just to test nature, but equally to try God. The period man invented mirror to see himself – And the moment his mirror mirrored his soiled soul.

Here was the moment in time man reduced his self-godlike-station to that of an earthworm – And was proud to call himself a hermaphrodite.

It was the time a few men claimed to be pregnant; when in truth they were not. Yes, the era such men drew public attention and became well-known.

It was that very decade when man tried to disprove God. Yes, the terrible days men became not only the agents of terror but ruled his fellow men with some terrible hands. This was the time men became gods. The time true happiness ceased. And in its place was the reign of petulance.

The age foreign parents were selling their new babies into the land. It was the age of adoptions – legal and illegal. And the days some of those babies were mercilessly slaughtered by some medical experts for their scientific experimentations. The age skin grafting, hearts' transplantations and even the stage of new brains' in-plants. It was the age of medical breakthroughs at the costs of others' lives – Mostly the babies' lives. An age fear ruled the world.

Yes, a season in time the Hippocratic Oath became an oath in and for hypocrisy. Indeed, the age of the restless spirits, bodies and souls. And a time, the unborn babies cried out and pleaded for their innocence. For sure, it was the sole season of mortal ecdysis of the immortal sources on high. And the brilliant moment man claimed ecesis on earth.

The period most people pretended to be taking it easy – while in truth the imperial works were in progress.

It was indeed the greatest period of individual prejudice, laxity and extreme hard-work. Indeed, here was the supreme moment that made men with less vision of mercies and total passions for instant gains.

Dreaming was the crowning factor of basic instinct. And those without it were viewed as laughing stocks. The period of lust and period of lack of it. The only moment in history men loved themselves alone.

True, the age was the apex of freedom as well as the zenith of selfishness. It was the only time of total temporary insanity in all men.

It was the decade the religious leaders thought and proclaimed the world would end. And to sum, the moment everything was crying out for a change.

It was a heartless stage in history, as well as a heart full of emotions – A surprising exhibition of deepest raw emotion and gruesome satanic sequence of the human soul. A soul without a savior; and a savior without a redeeming gene.

"Safe-practice" became the order of the time. It ruled virtually all things; medicine, sex, driving, talk; and even what popularly became known as "safe evangelism". Everyone was afraid of one thing or the other – Lest he be entangled in an unforeseeable litigation.

The hoodlums of the new society, the so-called "New Kingdom" set their baits and exploited the whole situation. The predators were viewed as a new plague. And they acted as such; "Tear them down" became their watch-word, their slogan, and a source of courage to their plague-like imagination.

The plagues plagued the land for a while. They preyed on the people, their properties, both in big, much so, in diverse and in much unsuspecting ways. The plagues were the "greedy little pooh" who were "little" in morality but too big in criminality. Morality was in chaos.

It was under this situation that Madam Cecilia jumped into the scene. She wanted a change, a total overhaul of the whole system starting from the church.

CHAPTER THIRTY

"Father, I've sinned" said the teenage girl.

"Welcome home my wayward child" said the new Priest. He kissed her. Then, he proceeded to touch the most sensitive parts of her body.

"Father, will I be able to also obtain God's pardon?" she asked the new man of God. The old one was on a sick leave. The much younger one was sent to the parish to minister to the people till the real Priest recovered.

"All your sins are wiped out, my dear girl. I promise" he replied still touching and sending out more explicit, non-verbal signals. She understood what the young Priest wanted. And she began to respond in kind. After all, he was in a position to yield to her desire for a divine pardon.

"Whatsoever ye shall bind on earth shall be bound in heaven, and whatsoever ye shall unbind on earth shall be unbound in heaven". So, the girl could not do without him.

She positioned herself. The man stood over. They began to make love. They did it for a while, dwelling on the taste of it. The new Priest was a good lover. He loved her and she loved him. He had promised and forgiven her the same sin three times in the past. Therefore, there was no reason for her to fear. After the encounter, she left, only to return the following day.

Madam Cecilia was telling the new Priest, Jacobien Sina what to preach on Sunday morning when the teenage girl rushed into the office. The older woman had a piece of paper and a pencil in her hands.

Pointing one line after another, she told him the new chronological order of church service designed by her advisory board; the way things would be done at the Universal Ecumenical Church; things to say, and things not to be said; things to do, and things not to be done. While she lectured, the young man nodded. She was a nonesuch in her emphatic piece of lecture.

It was obvious that the teenage girl, Melissa Ganus was displeased to see the two religious giants stand side by side.

"Madam Cecilia, I don't appreciate you standing up with my man" she warned the older woman. Since her sins were regularly forgiven through the intercession of the Priest, she would not tolerate any other woman, safe herself, coming closer to her source of forgiveness.

Madam Cecilia felt insulted. She would not take it.

"We don't take nonsense here, young lady" she rebuked.

"That's right" agreed the young Priest.

"Common Father, remember, haven't we done this before? Didn't you tell me God will forgive me?" Melissa addressed the new Priest. She walked flirtatiously to him and kissed him. He pushed her away.

"You've gotten me confused with someone else" the Priest protested.

"I'm not lying, Madam Cecilia; we've done it before on this desk, in this office. He told me 'all your sins are wiped out, my dear girl'". She addressed the woman instead of the Priest. She needed her verbal support. She didn't want her new love to deny her in the presence of another woman. "Please Father remember". This time she addressed the Priest.

"I don't know what this lunatic is talking about. Please Madam Cecilia; call the church security to remove this insane girl from here". The Priest denied the teenage girl's allegation, and he instructed his newest teacher on what to do to get rid of her – Get rid of his lover.

"Please, don't kick me out from your office" the young girl protested.

"You are insane. Do not come here again" shouted the young Priest as the security man dragged the girl out from his office.

CHAPTER THIRTY (B)

Reverend Johnson Gaye died of a massive heart attack when he heard that his relief Priest had defied his ministry. It was sin of fornication; a sin as hideous and as heavy as the adultery of his ex-wife.

Madam Cecilia was particularly infuriated at the whole turn of events that she vowed to take up the rein of the Priesthood. She saw herself entangled in the web of things. She personally went to the mission Hospital to tell the sick Priest how Jacobien Sina disgraced the entire church and the ministry.

"Though I die, from the grave shall I speak", were the last words the Priest said before he gave up the ghost. Madam Cecilia was there when he said those words. Seeing herself as a bearer of evil tiding, she felt a sense of guilt, a sad feeling that dwelt with her for the remaining days of her own life. It was this feeling, this close associating with the Priest's death; that unified and turned her into a crusader for the Priest's cause.

She called the press for an interview; paid the funeral home for the dead Priest's burial arrangement, and implored the members of the church to fix their sight on the church's challenges ahead. Besides, she had the fornicating Priest arrested; paid Melissa to charge the Priest for rape instead of sex by consent. She did.

When the people, mourners and press were gathered in the church, Madam Cecilia took the podium in a grand style. She looked like a possessed woman on a deadly mission. All the while, angry she looked. Mournful she was too.

A coffin carried by a team of six coffin-bearers on a pier was placed on a pair of pier-like benches. This, in the middle of the church. The Priest's widow, a recently married actress was bleeding with tears, uncontrollably beside the coffin. She was supported by a couple of hired mourners, 'true sympathizers' who held her from inflicting injuries on herself. Behind her were her relatives, movie-stars and other notable figures of her own rank – people who were ready to bear with her in the supreme moment of sorrow.

"This is time of female revolution", Madam Cecilia declared. She looked around her audience to see if there were any dissenting voice. There was none. So she continued. "Although we mourn the greatest loss in the entire Christian world, we must never, I say, never forget his dying words".

"What did he say?" a Priest in the midst who was from another parish questioned her without even raising his hand.

"He said, 'though I die, from the grave shall I speak'. I was the one who stood by him when he was dying. I was the one who heard him say his last words on this earth. It was a message addressed to none other than me. I am his new voice. I am his voice from the grave. Believe me, he shall speak". There was an applause. The mourners joined in the applause. The speaker noticed a faint grin on the widow's face.

"Yes", she continued "the time men ruled the world has come to an end. Therefore, it must be laid to rest…"

There followed a roaring murmur around, mostly by the men in the audience. The press and their camera-men were doing their own job, too. Cameras' flashlights flashing here and there.

Some of the women in the church's Rostrum smiled. But those who felt that it was the men's prerogative to rule took side with the men in the murmur of protest.

"I don't care how you feel, but understand we are united in our stand. Deborah was once a woman. She was chosen to lead despite in the numerous ego-conscious men in the land of Israel". The women who shared her views clapped their hands in an applause.

"Faith is our victory song" declared she. Then followed another applause.

"Ladies, we're going to hang in there till things turn around" another applause.

"God might be using the woman to shake us up" an old Priest at the back seat said. His hoarse voice was heard by the lady by the podium.

"Ladies, say 'Amen' to that".

"Amen" surprisingly everybody said so.

"The Female Messiah has come in the guise of a female preacher Madam Cecilia, you are the one" the same old Priest who made a remark, stood up, pointing at the lady by the podium and said.

"Church, say 'Amen' to that" Madam Cecilia commanded again.

"Amen" the people responded.

She was super-charged and ready to deliver. To her it was the right time to focus a laser-like intensity on the spiritual woes of the church.

Perhaps she was chosen by the Supreme Great Spirit to sweep the church from spiritual impurities, sacrileges, and tolerance of prejudice. A sultry-voiced woman, she delivered an emotional sermon which brought her audience too many a standing ovation and many a gut-wrenching emotional reaction.

At the end of the burial sermon, she noted in a chord that embodied the whole event. "Despite our current sorrow, the glory days are ahead of us".

CHAPTER THIRTY (C)

"With all their intelligence, they thought that I was rolling marijuana" cried the native Clarkwudoan, after the four members of the armed police force had beaten the food of the gods out from his brain.

"What happened, my dear man?" asked Madam Cecilia. She touched, like a caring mother, pretty affectionately at the beaten man. They knew each other. The man was her regular handyman.

"He is a man who does not know the difference between an offensive word and non-offensive word, yet he is in command of his police gang" the native man charged against the point-man of the other three police-men. The natives had a way with words in making other people see through their own points of view.

The man was on his way to his home. Walking, as he usually did, since he did not have enough money to buy an automobile. Those who drove by simply sped past by, simply because their God did not endow them with hearts rich in human seeds of kindness. Indeed, none of them had ever desired to give a poor, walking native fellow a lift or a ride in his or her luxurious automobile.

The natives were used to it. And whenever an automobile was coming, either in front or behind, they would simply walk deep into the bush…so as not to provoke the proud and arrogant owner of the automobile from crushing them with the automobile. After all, no progress-minded lawyer in the New Kingdom would desire to take on a case of the people that the wise Rulers of the land regarded as a bunch of primitive, half-human-beings.

A year before the encounter, the loving mother of the native man had a brush with a kindhearted new immigrant.

She was on her way from an open market, carrying her goods on her head.

Slowly, a new automobile, driven by a handsome man, stopped by. A glass window of the automobile quickly rolled down. This was followed by a very cordial greeting. With genuine smile all over his face, the man in the car opened his door and stepped out.

"Madam, I see you need a ride" the man said. Likely he was a rich, new immigrant, for his accent betrayed that.

Naturally, however, the elderly native lady who received his greeting became suspicious. It showed on her face. She stood still, looking at the young man who stopped by.

"Please enter into my car. I shall drive the car to where you are going". He opened the back door for her. When he wanted to convey her load away from her head, she refused. She was so intimidated by the neatness of the car that she refused to accept his help. Also, she was so intimidated by the neatness of the car that she refused an extended offer to put her goods in the car's booth. In fact, she carried her load on her head, sitting at the backseat while the man drove along. She was so fearful, so intimidated, like her own folks. Her son, the handyman, was a man.

The beaten man was not a user of marijuana. As she told Madam Cecilia before she hired him. He had never tasted that stuff since he was born. He was, in many ways, different from the other natives who used the strong weed in their religious communion.

He was on his way from his odd-job when a four-man team of police force arrested him on their own term.

"Aha! Primitive native, you won't get away with it this time" the leading police officer called out to him from their police car. The cruiser's red, blue and white lights rotating over head of the police cruiser.

"What are you talking about? Are you out of your mind?' the man on the sidewalk readdressed the insolent police officer.

"How dare that dirty dog insult me? Boys, get him" the police boss ordered his 'boys' to get the native fellow. They got out from their police cruiser and rushed towards the defenseless native fellow. They caught the poor native fellow and dragged him like a rag to their police boss. The police leader of the police men gave the native man a dirty slap on the face.

"It hurts, man. Why did you slap me?' the native man protested.

"I don't need to explain to you that you were about to inhale that marijuana" the policeman alleged an accusation against the native man.

"No, this is just a piece of paper, I rolled it up because I wanted to use it to clean up my itching ear, see" he showed the police officer a piece of a paper torn off from a daily newspaper. He also showed it to the other three police men.

"Even so, you wasted my time. And besides, you insulted a government official". He shouted 'you insulted a government official' at the native.

"Anyway, boys beat him up, so he will learn his lesson" the police boss ordered his three men. Quickly, they did as he ordered them. They used their batons and their hands on the man.

"Oh, this is a good exercise for the day" one of the police officers who was doing the job for which he was fabulously paid, said to his fellow police men.

"I've not beaten a primitive swine for a couple of weeks. Boss, thanks a million" said another police man.

"Yeah, I'm gonna enjoy it guys" yet, another police officer observed.

"Yes, it feels good to beat the hell out of these primitive folks. No! God forbid, primitive pigs I meant to say" the third policeman remarked.

"Boys, do as you wish. I'm going back to the car. When you are tired, you can come back to the car, we will drive off" the police boss said. Having given his 'boys' a go-ahead, he left for the car.

The native staggered and fell, yet the police officers continued to make his day. He cried. They laughed.

"If you die, we'll not even care to bury you" one of the officers mocked him.

CHAPTER THIRTY (D)

They had beaten him for more than fifteen minutes, sweating as they did their job, when a police siren echoed from a distance. Another gang of police men, for sure. Soon, a cabin of black-colored cars roared towards the street.

Five other police cruisers were systematically and in an alternate fashion leap-frogging one another. As they did, they closed every adjacent street that connected to the main highway. They blocked every car coming from the other streets which wanted to enter into the main street, being plied by the fleet of black-colored cars.

These fleet of cars were on their way to the cemetery or graveyard. The dead, of course was none other than the dead Priest. It was time for the burial.

Madam Cecilia was in the vehicle next to the first police cruiser. As soon as she saw the man who was being beaten by the police men, she recognized him.

"Clear and stop" she commanded her driver. He obeyed. She rushed out from the vehicle to the scene.

"Ijoquisor, oh my God, what's this?" she stopped the beating with her powerful presence. She was angry at what she saw. She knew the native to be a peaceful man.

"He was smoking pot" a police officer charged.

"That's not true" the woman contradicted the police man. The officers knew her and what she was capable of doing. "He never smokes".

"That's what he did" another police officer charged.

"Will you shut up your mouth? Tell the truth. What did he do?" she ordered. She looked at the three police men for an explanation. "Are you all dumb? What did he do to deserve this?"

"Ma'am I don't know".

"You don't know? You don't know, is that all you're going to say? Look, this is my own case. I'm taking up this case to the highest level. I will not give up until I see" then she began to point a finger at one of the three police officers after another "you, you and you turn in you badge. You know me…"

"Ma'am. Please don't do that to us, we were just obeying an order" the first police who laid a false accusation on the native pleaded.

"Whose order?" she questioned for an answer.

"The boss, in the car" the second police man pointed toward the cruiser.

"I am not going to take this nonsense" she walked straight to the officer in the car.

"Why?" she thundered.

"Oh Madam Cecilia, how are you?" he greeted her. She ignored his greeting and went straight to the heart of the matter.

"I asked you: why did you ask your men to beat this poor man?" she pointed at the bleeding native fellow.

"Oh Madam Cecilia, you know, we just wanted to have a good time" he smiled. She was seriously angry. He saw the expression on her face, and began to modify his statement, "Besides, he broke the law"

"What law?" she demanded.

"Why, he was about to smoke marijuana when we caught him, red-handed, you know" answered the police boss.

"I don't know. Any proof?" she questioned.

"I can assure you…"

"Show me the proof. Now" Madam Cecilia demanded.

"Oh, why in such a hurry?" he said. And he got pretty irritated, because he did not want to lose his job, either.

"I know you don't have any excuse for beating that man; you did it because you thought he had no one to defend his case. But from now on, rest informed that I will not go to sleep until I see that justice is served". With that she left the policeman to digest the weight of her statements.

"Thank you for this. I don't know how to repay you" the beaten man told the woman.

"You don't have to thank me. You are innocent. They had no right to treat you the way they did" responded Madam Cecilia. She was now in the limousine with the native man sitting beside her. She liked him despite the overall prejudice the society held against the natives.

"I'm not lying" continued the native man. "One day at Millionaire Highway Park, two kids came to a man mowing the city lawn and asked him to sell them some grass. The man told them to go and come back. Soon after they left, he took some of the grass from his mowing machine, wrapped them up in some torn newspapers. When the kids came back, he sold the grass to them for ten hatums. The kids took it and came back sometime later and told him that it was good".

"They thought he sold them marijuana, the man who did that was wise" said Madam Cecilia.

"I don't have good luck with money" the native man said. "But I'm glad that I don't spend twenty hatums for cut grass. My wife died that way. She spent all her money, her mother's money and all my money to buy grass. But she wouldn't allow me to buy two bottles of beer" he said.

The woman, Madam Cecilia laughed. And while she was laughing, she looked at the face of her friend, the handyman:

"I'm not laughing at you, though" she said. Excusing herself from her laughter.

"I know. How can you? Was it not you who saved my life from the hands of those wolves in police clothes?" replied the handyman with a thoughtful question.

"You see, that's what we've been talking about. Those boys who bought those grasses were kids of the rich men. The law does not touch them. Here you are, an innocent man, beaten up just because you are different" said Madam Cecilia.

"He called me a primitive native" the native fellow told her.

"Did he?" asked Madam Cecilia.

"Yes" replied the native man.

"Who did? I wanna know the very one".

"Their leader, the cop".

"He will not get away with it" she pledged.

CHAPTER THIRTY-ONE

By the grave side a squeaky sound coming from inside the grave was heard. The sound was distinct, explicit, graphic and even very romantic.

"What's happening inside there?" a burier asked.

"I don't know" a police officer replied.

"Let's see" he peeped inside. Behold, two insane couple were making love inside the newly dug grave.

"Run away from our house" the male partner in the grave demanded.

"Get out from there you fools. This grave is not only your house, it will be your grave too if you don't come out now" the policeman demanded.

"Romance is a dog-game, you fall for me, then I fall for you" replied the naked insane man in the grave.

"Don't push me into marrying a prostitute. You hear me? I won't say it again if your ears are in your moon" the female one said after that.

By this time, many people were looking at the couple in the grave. To their surprise, the woman in the grave took a lump of the grave soil and threw it at the policeman. The lump missed its target by a few inches.

"What shall we do? Leave this and dig another? Twice the original price, because it's now emergency'" asked the chief burier.

There were three of them, professional buriers, they were.

"Ask the widow" the police office held the burier's hand to stop him. "You better ask Madam Cecilia. She is in charge".

Madam Cecilia drew nearer to the gravesite. Unusual scene. People were looking inside the grave.

"What's happening? Why is everybody looking inside the grave? Is it not deep enough?" asked Madam Cecilia.

"Ma'am, please look inside" the police officer told her. She did.

"Who are you looking inside my kitchen, don't you have any shame?" the naked woman inside the grave addressed her. To support her claim, she grabbed a lump of grave soil, ready to throw it at the intruder who was looking inside her 'kitchen'. Quickly, Madam Cecilia withdrew from the gravesite.

"Ma'am, what shall we do, dig anther grave?" the chief burier asked. Madam Cecilia.

"How much?" Madam Cecilia asked him.

"Twice the original price. It's emergency. There is nothing we can do about it" the greedy chief burier presented her with his sales' pitch.

"That's silly, pull those idiots from the grave" she commanded. The police officer blew a whistle. Within a minute ten other police men converged to the gravesite, ready for a command performance.

"Bring them out" he ordered his men. One after another, the police men jumped inside the grave. A fight followed up. The mad people were not willing to give in. They clawed, slapped and bit any of the officers who tried to touch them.

Three of the officers were bleeding from the wounds inflicted on them by the crazy couple's teeth.

"Gag them and drag them out" the officer outside the grave commanded those inside the grave. They did.

When they succeeded in bringing out the naked, mad couple from the grave, the people in the cemetery drew nearer to see them. While this was happening, the naked woman extricated herself from two police men – And rushed back and jumped inside the grave – Her kitchen.

"You can't remove from my house" she dared the police officers from inside. Five police officers ran after her. She seemed much more energetic than her man. She continued to fight. As the men tried to re-gag her, she grabbed a hold on a policeman's baton. While another struggled to disentangle the other's baton from her hand, she let go. With a terrifying speed, she yanked a pistol from the policeman's waist. Without blinking an eye, she corked and released three rounds of gunshots. Down fell one of the police officers at her feet. Dead. There was a stampede.

The commanding officer, seeing what she did, pulled out his own pistol and blew the insane woman's brain away. Later, her body and the body of the police officer who she killed were pulled out from the grave.

The ceremonial songs and prayers were avoided before the Priest's body was laid to rest. A tombstone with his dying words inscribed on it was placed on the tomb. That, after the burial, towards the head position of the gravesite.

The inscription, the Priest's parting words were engraved on a marble tombstone. It read, "Though I die, from the grave shall I speak".

CHAPTER THIRTY-TWO

When Madam Cecilia returned from the burial ceremony, she paid an unscheduled visit to her next palace neighbor, the Duke, the leader of the New Kingdom. The aging Monarch was not surprised to see her. Because they were good friends. She had, in the past, helped him solve some mysterious problems – Mainly, revealing those who were secret agitators in his administration.

Of course, he dealt with the potential troublemakers with a heavy hand. In return, he helped her build up her business. That was more than ten years ago. Years after the school children disturbed peace and tranquility of his Kingdom.

Madam Cecilia was what someone would regard as the Duke's true friend; the only person the Duke dared to trust. They knew each other. He loved power. And she loved money, mysteries, intrigues, witchcraft and association with people in position of influence. Though she held no elective political post, her personal clout in the Kingdom was enormous.

She and her host talked in a low key. She bared her soul before the man – Expressing her dreams for the New Kingdom; her hope for the future; her desire for racial harmony; and her longing for perpetual peace when their stay on the earth was over.

She told him her experience in the Universal Ecumenical Church. The need to use religion to promote true peace, not a hypocritical one. The need to get the women involved in all the affairs of the kingdom.

As the Duke listened with rapt attention, she narrated the incidence of police brutality. She went ahead to add that such was not just an isolated case, but a clear reflection of pure lawlessness of those who were supposed to be on the side of the law.

She told him how some law caretakers had often planted crimes, just to indict those they did not really like. And in due time, tortured the innocents.

She advised the crown to do something about the oppressed, the untouchables, the voiceless remnants, and to overhaul the entire system in a dramatic way. She told him that the time was ripe for a change.

There was a subdued rage on the face of the aging monarch.

"I didn't know it was this grave" said the aging Monarch.

"It is worse. One in your position may not be privileged to lead the experience" said Madam Cecilia.

"That is true" the Monarch agreed with Madam Cecilia.

"Do you know there are those who still live in caves and chained forests in this kingdom?" she asked the Duke.

"God forbid! Where? Such cannot be" the Duke felt a sense of spite.

"I don't mean to hurt your ego, your majesty. However, I must bring the truth before you. I am your friend, no matter how bad they are…" she declared, confidently.

"I have a supreme confidence in you. You can count on that. Now it appears my cabinet officials are only interested in building up a fine public image here before me, and in overseas, leaving our dirty linens forever unwashed" the Duke said.

"Your majesty, I shall forever appreciate your great confidence in me. I shall always do my best, going more than an extra mile, extra length, to show that I am worthy of such a majestic trust. Sir, you are right about your cabinet. I trust they are only fearful to face you with the facts…"

"Fearful for what?" the Duke asked her. His voice was louder than usual; eyebrows raised.

"They are fearful for their jobs; yes even their lives. I am your friend, I must not hide these facts from you…"

"I see. Thank you, you are indeed a true friend. I wish I had one or two members of my cabinet who were as courageous as you are. Forget that. I'm glad you are the only person in the vast Kingdom, I could look in her face and tell her that I trust her wholeheartedly" said the Monarch.

"Thank you, your majesty" she thanked him.

CHAPTER THIRTY-THREE

From the New Kingdom's Central Television Center, the Duke made a far reaching pledge and a call for a paramount duty.

He made the speech just two days after the "Female Messiah's" visit. And below is the Monarch's holy speech in its entirety.

> "Today I declare a war on racism. We shall sacrifice everything it takes to win this war. I've resolved to call on all our armed men. Members of the police force, the Imperial Warriors, National Security Agencies and the entire populace at large to move forward to the battle before us.
>
> Our armed men will receive a new training. It will not be a training to kill their foes in the warfronts, but a training of the mind. A training to accept one's enemies as friends; a training to accept the untouchables as friends; a

training to have a classless culture, a Kingdom rich in pure love and compassion.

We shall turn our weapons of war into weapons of love. We pledge to love one another irrespective of our differences.

We pledge to see this battle won first in our Kingdom before we would even think of spreading this sound idea abroad.

This is our duty, our mission and our goal. Ahead you must go into the war-front. With valor, you must head to the urgent victory. I have a great confidence in all our people, in our ability to march confidently forward, in our uniqueness of purpose and with our souls firmly fixed till the crown of victory is ours. Thank you, Thank you my people. Yes, I say to you all, thank you once again".

The speech was brief, subdued in tone and direct to the point. It was a speech that focused on the paramount issue of the day: War against all kinds of human prejudice.

Here was an old Monarch whose primary indulgence, simply put, was to continue to enjoy his conquests in his old age, on a new course. With the new challenge, though age-old, became his passion. He was known for his determination. His patience had been tested prior to this, and proven worthy of his station. As he made his pledge in the speech, there was no going back.

His was a speech, a far-cry destined to usher in a new era in the New Kingdom. "Nothing with a beginning is without an end" the Duke told the Female Messiah before she left his palace, after the visit two days ago.

He favored her wishes. The Kingdom would now see many changes, and at last live in peace and pure harmony.

OGWUSIWO!!!

www.ingramcontent.com/pod-product-compliance
Lightning Source LLC
LaVergne TN
LVHW021800060526
838201LV00058B/3170